THE
ADVENTURE
CLUB AFLOAT

Ralph Henry Barbour

The Adventure Club Afloat

Ralph Henry Barbour

© 1st World Library – Literary Society, 2004
PO Box 2211
Fairfield, IA 52556
www.1stworldlibrary.org
First Edition

LCCN: 2005901374

Softcover ISBN: 1-4218-1176-6
Hardcover ISBN: 1-4218-1076-X
eBook ISBN: 1-4218-1276-2

Purchase *"The Adventure Club Afloat"*
as a traditional bound book at:
www.1stWorldLibrary.org/purchase.asp?ISBN=1-4218-1176-6

1st World Library Literary Society is a nonprofit
organization dedicated to promoting literacy by:

- Creating a free internet library accessible from any
  computer worldwide.
- Hosting writing competitions and offering book
  publishing scholarships.

The Adventure Club Afloat
contributed by Tim, Ed & Rodney
in support of
1st World Library Literary Society

CHAPTER I

HOW IT STARTED

The Adventure Club had its inception, one evening toward the last of June, in Number 17 Sumner Hall, which is the oldest, most vine-hidden and most hallowed of the seven dormitories of Dexter Academy. It was a particularly warm evening, the two windows were wide open and the green-shaded light on the study table in the centre of the room had been turned low - Sumner prided itself on being conservative to the extent of gas instead of electricity and tin bathtubs instead of porcelain - and in the dim radiance the three occupants of the room were scarcely more than darker blurs.

Since final examinations had ended that afternoon and Graduation Day was only some twenty-eight hours away, none of the three was doing anything more onerous than yawning, and the yawn which came from Perry Bush, didn't sound as though it cost much of an effort. It was, rather, a comfortable, sleepy yawn, one that expressed contentment and relief, a sort of "Glad-that's-over-and-I'm-still-alive" yawn.

There was a window-seat under each casement in Number 17, and each was occupied by a recumbent figure. Perry was on the right-hand seat, his hands under his head and one foot sprawled on the floor, and Joe Ingersoll was in the other, his slim, white-trousered legs jack-knifed against the darker square of the open window. Near Joe, his feet tucked sociably against Joe's ribs, Steve Chapman, the third of the trio, reclined in a Morris chair. I use the word reclined advisedly, for Steve had lowered the back of the chair to its last notch, and to say that he was sitting would require a stretch of the imagination almost as long as Steve himself! Through the windows Steve could see the dark masses of the campus elms, an occasional star between the branches, and, by raising his head the fraction of an inch, the lights in the upper story of Hawthorne, across the yard. Somewhere under the trees outside a group of fellows were singing to the accompaniment of a wailing ukelele. They sang softly, so that the words floated gently up to the open casements just distinguishable:

> *"Years may come and years may go,*
> *Seasons ebb and seasons flow,*
> *Autumn lie 'neath Winters' snow,*
> *Spring bring Summer verdancy.*
> *Life may line our brow with care,*
> *Time to silver turn our hair,*
> *Still, to us betide whate'er,*
> *Dexter, we'll remember thee!*
>
> *"Other memories may fade,*
> *Hopes grow dim in ev'ning's shade,*
> *Golden friendships that we made -"*

"Aw, shut up!" muttered Perry, breaking the silence that had held them for several minutes. Joe Ingersoll laughed softly.

"You don't seem to like the efforts of the - um - sweet-voiced choristers," he said in his slow way.

"I don't like the sob-stuff," replied Perry resentfully. "What's the use of rubbing it in? Why not let a fellow be cheerful after he has got through by the skin of his teeth and kicked his books under the bed? Gosh, some folks never want anyone to be happy!" He raised himself by painful effort and peered out and down into the gloom. "Sophs, I'll bet," he murmured, falling back again on the cushions. "No one else would sit out here on the grass and sing school songs two days before the end. I hope that idiot singing second bass will get a brown-tail caterpillar down his neck!"

RALPH HENRY BARBOUR

"The end!" observed Steve Chapman. "You say that as if we were all going to die the day after tomorrow, Perry! Cheer up! Vacation's coming!"

"Vacation be blowed!" responded Perry. "What's that amount to, anyway? Nothing ever happens to me in vacation. It's all well enough for you fellows to laugh. You're going up to college together in the Fall. I'm coming back to this rotten hole all alone!"

"Not quite alone, Sweet Youth," corrected Joe. "There will be some four hundred other fellows here."

"Oh, well, you know what I mean," said Perry impatiently. "You and Steve will be gone, and I don't give a hang for any other chaps!"

He ended somewhat defiantly, conscious that he had indulged in a most unmanly display of sentiment, and was glad that the darkness hid the confusion and heightened colour that followed the confession. Steve and Joe charitably pretended not to have noticed the lamentable exhibition of feeling, and a silence followed, during which the voices of the singers once more became audible.

> *"Dexter! Mother of our Youth!*
> *Dexter! Guardian of the Truth!"*

"*Cut it out!*" Perry leaned over the windowsill and bawled the command down into the darkness. A defiant jeer answered him.

"Don't be fresh," said Steve reprovingly. Perry mumbled and relapsed into silence. Presently, sighing as he changed his position, Joe said:

"I believe Perry's right about vacation, Steve. Nothing much ever does happen to a fellow in Summer. I believe I've had more fun in school than at home the last six years."

The others considered the statement a minute. Then: "Correct," said Steve. "It's so, I guess. We're always crazy to get home in June and just as crazy to get back to school again in September, and I believe we all have more good times here than at home."

"Of course we do," agreed Perry animatedly. "Anyway, I do. Summers are all just the same. My folks lug me off to the Water Gap and we stay there until it's time to come back here. I play tennis and go motoring and sit around on the porch and - and - bathe -"

"Let's hope so," interpolated Joe gravely.

"And nothing really interesting ever happens," ended Perry despairingly. "Gee, I'd like to be a pirate or - or something!"

"Summers *are* rather deadly," assented Steve. "We go to the seashore, but the place is filled with swells, and about all they do is change their clothes, eat and sleep. When you get ready for piracy, Perry, let me know, will you! I'd like to sign-on."

"Put me down, too," said Joe. "I've always had a - um - sneaking idea that I'd make a bully pirate. I'm naturally bloodthirsty and cruel. And I've got a mental list of folks who - um - I'd like to watch walk the plank!"

"Fellows of our ages have a rotten time of it, anyway," Perry grumbled. "We're too old to play kids' games and too young to do anything worth while. What I'd like to do -"

"Proceed, Sweet Youth," Joe prompted after a moment.

"Well, I'd like to - to start something! I'd like to get away somewhere and do things. I'm tired of loafing around in white flannels all day and keeping my hands clean. And I'm tired of dabbing whitewash on my shoes! Didn't you fellows ever think that you'd like to get good and dirty and not have to care?

Wouldn't you like to put on an old flannel shirt and a pair of khaki trousers and some 'sneakers' and - and roll in the mud?"

"Elemental stuff," murmured Joe. "He's been reading Jack London."

"Well, that's the way I feel, lots of times," said Perry defiantly. "I'm tired of being clean and white, and I'm tired of dinner jackets, and I'm sick to death of hotel porches! Gee, a healthy chap never was intended to lead the life of a white poodle with a pink ribbon around his neck! Me for some rough-stuff!"

"You're dead right, too," agreed Steve. "That kind of thing is all right for Joe, of course. Joe's a natural-born 'fusser.' He's never happier than when he's dolled up in a sport-shirt and a lavender scarf and toasting marshmallows. But -"

"Is that so?" inquired Joe with deep sarcasm. "If I was half the 'fusser' you are -"

"What I want," interrupted Perry, warming to his theme, "is adventure! I'd like to hunt big game, or discover the North Pole -"

"You're a year or two late," murmured Joe.

"- or dig for hidden treasure!"

"You should - um - change your course of reading," advised Joe. "Too much Roosevelt and Peary and Stevenson is your trouble. Read the classics for awhile - or the Patty Books."

"That's all right, but you chaps are just the same, only you won't own up to it."

"One of us will," said Steve; "and does."

"Make it two," yawned Joe. "Beneath this - um - this polished exterior there beats a heart - I mean there flows the red blood of -"

"Look here, fellows, why not?" asked Steve.

"Why not what?" asked Perry.

"Why not have adventures? They say that all you have to do is look for them."

"Don't you believe it! I've looked for them for years and I've never seen one yet." Perry swung his feet to the floor and sat up.

"Well, not at Delaware Water Gap, naturally. You've got to move around, son. You don't find them by sitting all day with your feet on the rail of a hotel piazza."

"Where do you find them, then?" Perry demanded.

Steve waved a hand vaguely aloft into the greenish radiance of the lamp. "All round. North, east, south and west. Land or sea. Adventures, Perry, are for the adventurous. Now, here we are, three able-bodied fellows fairly capable of looking after ourselves in most situations, tired of the humdrum life of Summer resorts. What's to prevent our spending a couple of months together and finding some adventures? Of course, we can't go to Africa and shoot lions and wart-hogs - whatever they may be, - and we can't fit out an Arctic exploration party and discover Ingersoll Land or Bush Inlet or Chapman's Passage, but we could have a mighty good time, I'd say, and, even if we didn't have many hair-breadth escapes, I'll bet it would beat chasing tennis balls and doing the Australian crawl and keeping our white shoes and trousers clean!"

"We could be as dirty as we liked!" sighed Perry ecstatically. "Lead me to it!"

"It sounds positively fascinating," drawled Joe, "but just how would we go about it? My folks, for some unfathomable reason, think quite a lot of me, and I don't just see them letting me amble off like that; especially in - um - such disreputable company."

"I should think they'd be glad to be rid of you for a Summer," said Perry. "Anyhow, let's make believe it's possible, fellows, and talk about it."

"Why isn't it possible?" asked Steve. "My folks would raise objections as well as yours, Joe, but I guess I could fetch them around. After all, there's no more danger than in staying at home and trying to break your neck driving an automobile sixty miles an hour. Let's really consider the scheme, fellows. I'm in earnest. I want to do it. What Perry said is just what I've been thinking without saying. Why, hang it, a fellow needs something of the sort to teach him sense and give him experience. This thing of hanging around a hotel porch all Summer makes a regular mollycoddle of a fellow. I'm for revolt!"

"Hear! Hear!" cried Perry enthusiastically. "Revolution! *A bas la* Summer Resort! *Viva* Adventure!"

"Shut up, idiot! Do you really mean it, Steve, or are you just talking? If you mean it, I'm with you to the last - um - drop of blood, old chap! I've always wanted to revolt about something, anyway. One of my ancestors helped throw the English breakfast tea into Boston Harbour. But I don't want to get all het up about this unless there's really something in it besides jabber."

"We start the first day of July," replied Steve decisively.

"Where for?"

"That is the question, friends. Shall it be by land or sea?"

"Land," said Joe.

"Sea," said Perry.

"The majority rules and I cast my vote with Perry. Adventures are more likely to be found on the water, I think, and it's adventures we are looking for."

"But I always get seasick," objected Joe. "And when I'm seasick you couldn't tempt me with any number of adventures. I simply - um - don't seem to enthuse much at such times."

"You can take a lemon with you," suggested Perry cheerfully. "My grandmother -"

Joe shook his head. "They don't do you any good," he said sadly.

"Don't they! My grandmother -"

"Bother your grandmother! How do we go to sea, Steve? Swim or - or how?"

"We get my father's cruiser," replied Steve simply. "She's a forty-footer and togged out like an ocean-liner. Has everything but a swimming-pool. She -"

"Nix on the luxuries," interrupted Perry. "The simple life for me. Let's hire an old moth-eaten sailboat -"

"Nothing doing, Sweet Youth! If I'm to risk my life on the heaving ocean I want something under me. Besides, being seasick is rotten enough, anyhow, without having to roll around in the cock-pit of a two-by-twice sailboat. That cruiser listens well, Steve, but - um - will papa fall for it? If it was my father -"

"I think he will," answered Steve seriously. "Dad doesn't have much chance to use the boat himself, and this Summer he's likely to be in the city more than ever. The trouble is that the *Cockatoo* is almost too big for three of us to handle."

"Oh, piffle!"

"It's so, though. I know the boat, Perry. She's pretty big when it comes to making a landing or picking up a mooring. If we were all fairly good seamen it might be all right, but I wouldn't want to try to handle the *Cockatoo* without a couple of sailors aboard."

"I once sailed a knockabout," said Perry.

"And I had a great-grandfather who was a sea captain," offered Joe encouragingly. "What price great-grandfather?"

"Don't see where your grandfather and Perry's grandmother come into this," replied Steve. "How would it do if we gathered up two or three other fellows? The *Cockatoo* will accommodate six."

"Who could we get?" asked Joe dubiously.

"Neil Fairleigh, for one."

"How about Han?" offered Joe.

"Hanford always wants to boss everything," objected Perry.

"He knows boats, though, and so does Neil," said Steve. "And they're both good fellows. That would make five of us, and five isn't too many. We can't afford to hire a cook, you know; at least, I can't; and someone will have to look after that end of it. Who can cook?"

"I can't!" Perry made the disclaimer with great satisfaction.

"No more can I," said Joe cheerfully. "Let Neil be cook."

"I guess we'll all have to take a try at it. I dare say any of us can fry an egg and make coffee; and you can buy almost everything ready to eat nowadays."

"Tell you who's a whale of a cook," said Perry eagerly. "That's Ossie Brazier. Remember the time we camped at Mirror Lake last Spring? Remember the flapjacks he made? M-mm!"

"I didn't go," said Steve. "What sort of a chap is Brazier? I don't know him very well."

"Well, Oscar's one of the sort who will do anything just as long as he thinks he doesn't have to," replied Joe. "If we could get him to come along and tell him that he - um - simply must *not* ask to do the cooking, why - there you are!"

"Merely a matter of diplomacy," laughed Steve. "Well, we might have Brazier instead of Hanford - or Neil."

"Why not have them all if the boat will hold six?" asked Joe. "Seems to me the more we have the less each of us will have to do. I mean," he continued above the laughter, "that - um - a division of labour -"

"We get you," said Perry. "But, say, I wish you'd stop talking about it, fellows. I'm going to be disappointed when I wake up and find it's only a bright and gaudy dream."

"It isn't a dream," answered Steve, "unless you say so. I'll go, and I'll guarantee to get the *Cockatoo* without expense other than the cost of running her. If you and Joe can get your folks to let you come, and we can get hold of, say, two other decent chaps to fill the crew, why, we'll do it!"

"Do you honestly mean it?" demanded Perry incredulously. "Gee, I'll get permission if I have to - to go without it!"

"How about you, Joe?"

"Um - I guess I could manage it. How long would we be gone?"

"A month. Two, if you like. Start the first of July, or as soon

RALPH HENRY BARBOUR

after as possible, and get back in August."

"How much would it cost us?" inquired Perry. "I'm not a millionaire like you chaps."

"Wouldn't want to say offhand. We'd have to figure that. That's another reason for filling the boat up, though. The more we have the less everyone's share of the expense will be."

"Let's have the whole six, then, for money's scarce in my family these days. Let's make it a club, fellows. The Club of Six, or something of that sort. It sounds fine!"

"Take in another fellow and call it The Lucky Seven," suggested Joe.

"We might not be lucky, though," laughed Steve. "I'll tell you a better name."

"Shoot!"

"The Adventure Club."

CHAPTER II

THE CLUB GROWS

And that is the way in which it happened. It began in fun and ended quite seriously. They sat up in Number 17 Sumner until long after bedtime that night, figuring the cost of the expedition, planning the cruise, even listing supplies. The more they talked about it the more their enthusiasm grew. Perry was for having Steve send a night message then and there to his father asking for the boat, but Steve preferred to wait until he reached home and make the request by word of mouth.

"He would just think I was fooling or crazy if I telegraphed," he explained. "Tomorrow we'll try to dig up three other fellows to go along, and then, as soon as we all get home, we'll find out whether our folks will stand for it. You must all telegraph me the first thing. Don't wait to write, because I must know as soon as possible. I dare say there's work to be done on the *Cockatoo* before she's ready for the water, and we don't want to have to wait around until the end of July. The fun of doing anything is to do it right off. If you wait you lose half the pleasure. Now you'd better beat it, Perry. It's after ten. If you meet a proctor close your eyes and make believe you're walking in your sleep."

Perry reached his own room, on the floor above, without being sighted, however, and subsequently spent a sleepless hour in joyous anticipation of at last finding some of those adventures that all his life he had longed for. And when he did at length fall asleep it was to have the most outlandish dreams, visions in

RALPH HENRY BARBOUR

which he endured shipwreck, fought pirates and was all but eaten by cannibals. The most incongruous phase of the dream, as recollected on waking, was that the *Cockatoo* had been, not a motor-boat at all, but a trolley-car! He distinctly remembered that the pirates, on boarding it, had each dropped a nickel in the box!

Fortunately for the success of the Adventure Club, the next morning held no duties. In the afternoon the deciding baseball game was to be played, but, except for gathering belongings together preliminary to packing, nothing else intervened between now and the graduation programme of the morrow. Hence it was an easy matter to hold what might be termed the first meeting of the club. Besides the originators there were present Messrs. Fairleigh, Hanford and Brazier. After Steve had locked the door to prevent interruption, he presented to the newcomers a summary of the scheme. It was received with enthusiasm and unanimous approval, but Neil Fairleigh and Oscar Brazier sadly admitted that in their cases parental permission was extremely doubtful. George Hanford, whose parents were dead and who was under the care of a guardian, thought that in his case there would be no great difficulty. The other two viewed him a trifle enviously. Then, because one may always hope, they had to hear the particulars and each secretly began to fashion arguments to overcome the objections at home. Finally Oscar Brazier inquired interestedly:

"Who is going to cook for you?"

"Oh, we'll take turns, maybe," answered Joe. "Or we might hire a cook."

Joe stole a look at Steve. Oscar only shuffled his feet.

"I say hire," remarked Perry. "Any of us could do it after a fashion, I dare say, but you get frightfully hungry on the water and need good stuff well cooked, and lots of it."

"Yes," agreed Steve, "any of us would make an awful mess of

it. Cooking's an art."

Oscar cleared his throat and frowned. "You'd have to pay a lot for a cook," he said. "It isn't hard, really. I could do it - if I were going along."

"That's so," George Hanford confirmed. But the rest seemed unflatteringly doubtful. The silence was almost embarrassing. At last Joe said hurriedly:

"Well, we don't have to decide that now. Besides, if you can't come with us - um -" His voice trailed off into a relieved silence. Oscar smiled haughtily.

"That's all right," he said. "If you prefer a cook, say so. Only, if I did go I'd be willing to do the cooking, and I'll bet I could do it as well as any cook you could hire. Isn't it so, Han?"

"Yes, I call you a mighty nifty cook, Ossie. I've eaten your biscuits more than once. Flapjacks, too."

"Well," said Joe politely, "camp cooking is um - different, I guess, from regular cooking. Of course, I don't say Ossie couldn't do it, mind you, but - we wouldn't want to take chances. On the whole, I think it would be best to have a regular cook."

"We might let Ossie try it," suggested Perry judicially.

"Oh, I'm not crazy about it," disclaimed Oscar, piqued. "If you prefer to pay out good money for a cook -"

"Not at all," interrupted Steve soothingly. "We want to do the whole thing as cheaply as we can. I see no harm in leaving the cooking end of it to you, Brazier; that is, if you can go."

"I'm going to make a big try for it," declared Oscar resolutely. "If my folks won't let me, they - they'll wish they had!"

Whereupon, emboldened by Oscar's stand, Neil Fairleigh expressed the conviction that he, too, could manage it some way. "I dare say that if I tell my dad that all you chaps are going he will think it's all right. It wouldn't be for all Summer, anyway, would it?"

"The idea now," responded Steve, "is to start out for a month's cruise and extend it if we cared to. I suppose any of us that got tired could quit after the month was up." He smiled. "We'd all have to sign-on for a month, though."

"Right-o," agreed Hanford. "What about electing officers? Oughtn't we to do that? Someone ought to be in charge, I should think."

"Sure!" exclaimed Joe. "We'll ballot. Throw that pad over here, Ossie."

"Wait a minute," said Steve. "I've been thinking, fellows. The *Cockatoo* will hold six comfortably. The main cabin has berths for four and the owner's cabin for two, but if I'm not mistaken the berths in the owner's cabin are extension, and if they are we could bunk three fellows in there, or even four at a pinch. That would give us room for seven or eight in all. Eight might make it a bit crowded, but she's a big, roomy boat and I think we could do with seven fellows all right. And seven's a lucky number, too. So suppose we take in one more while we're at it?"

"The more the merrier," agreed Joe. "Who have you got in mind?"

Steve shook his head. "No one, but I guess we can think of a fellow. There's -"

Steve was interrupted by a knock on the door, and when Hanford, who was nearest, had, at a nod from Steve, unlocked the portal a tall, rather serious-faced youth of seventeen entered.

"Oh, am I butting-in?" he asked. "I didn't know. I'll come back later, Joe." Philip Street smiled apologetically and started a retreat, but Steve called him back.

"Hold on, Phil!" he cried. "Come in here. You're the very fellow we want. Close the door and find a seat, will you?"

"By Jove, that's so!" exclaimed Joe, and the others heartily endorsed him. Oddly enough, not one would have thought of Phil Street in all probability, but each recognised the fact that he was the ideal fellow to complete the membership. Steve, Joe aiding and the others attempting to, outlined the plan. If they had expected signs of enthusiasm from Phil they were doomed to disappointment, for that youth listened silently and attentively until they had ended and then asked simply:

"When are you planning to get away?"

"As near the first of the month as we can," replied Steve.

"I'm afraid I couldn't go, then," said Phil. "I'm a delegate to the C.B. Convention, you see, and that doesn't end until the sixth."

"I'd forgotten that," said Joe disappointedly.

"What's C.B. stand for?" inquired Hanford.

"Christian Brotherhood," supplied Steve. "Look here, Phil, could you go after the sixth?"

"Yes, I'd love to, thanks."

"All right then, you're signed-on. If we get away before that we'll pick you up somewhere. If we don't you can start with us. How is that?"

"Quite satisfactory," answered Phil.

RALPH HENRY BARBOUR

"But are you sure your folks will let you?" asked Perry.

"Oh, yes, I spend my Summers about as I like."

"Think of that!" sighed Perry. "Gee, I wish my folks were like that."

"I guess," said Steve, "that Phil's folks know he won't get into trouble, Perry, while yours are pretty certain that you will. It makes a difference. Now we can go ahead with that election, can't we? How about nominations?"

"No need of them," declared Joe. "What officers do we want?"

"Well, this is a club - the Adventure Club, Phil, is the name we've chosen - and so I suppose we ought to have a president and a vice-president and -"

"Rot!" said Perry. "Too high-sounding. Let's elect a captain and a treasurer and let it go at that."

"I never heard of a club having a captain," Oscar Brazier objected.

"Nor anyone else," agreed Joe. "Let's follow the Nihilist scheme and elect a Number One, a Number Two and a Number Three. Number One can be the boss, a sort of president, you know, Number Two can correspond to a vice-president and Number Three can be secretary and treasurer. How's that?"

"Suits me," said Steve. "Tear up some pieces of paper, Perry. We'll each vote for the three officers, writing the names in order, then the fellow getting the most votes - "

"I don't know as I ought to vote," said Neil Fairleigh, "because I'm not sure I can go. Maybe I'd better not, eh?"

"Oh, shucks, never mind that," replied Perry. "You can join

the club, anyway, and be a sort of non-resident member. Here you are, fellows. Who's got a pen or something?"

During the ensuing two or three minutes there was comparative silence in Number 17, and while the seven occupants of the room busy themselves with pens or pencils let us look them over since we are likely to spend some time in their company from now on.

First of all there is Steve Chapman, seventeen years of age, a tall, well-built and nicely proportioned youth with black hair and eyes, a quick, determined manner and an incisive speech. Steve was Football Captain last Fall. Next him sits George Hanford. Han, as the boys call him, is eighteen, also a senior, and also a football player. He is big and rangey, good-natured and popular, and is president of the senior class.

Joe Ingersoll's age is seventeen. He is Steve's junior by two months. He is of medium height, rather thin, light complexioned and has peculiarly pale eyes behind the round spectacles he wears. Joe is first baseman on the Nine, and a remarkably competent one. He is slow of speech and possesses a dry humour that on occasion can be uncomfortably ironical. Beside him, Perry Bush is a complete contrast, for Perry is large-limbed, rather heavy of build, freckle-faced, red-haired and jolly. He has very dark blue eyes and, in spite of a moon-shaped countenance, is distinctly pleasing to look at; he is sixteen.

Neil Fairleigh and Phil Street are of an age, seventeen, but in other regards are quite unalike. Neil is of medium height, with his full allowance of flesh, and has hair the hue of new rope and grey-blue eyes. He is even-tempered, easy-going and, if truth must be told, somewhat lazy. Phil Street is quite tall, rather thin and dark complexioned, a nice-looking, somewhat serious youth whose infrequent smile is worth waiting for. He is an Honor Man, a distinction attained by no other member of our party save Steve. The last of the seven is Oscar Brazier, and Ossie, as the boys call him, is sixteen years old, short and square, strongly-made and conspicuous for neither beauty nor scholarly attainments. Ossie has a snub nose, a lot of rebellious brown hair, red cheeks and a wide mouth that is usually smiling. Renowned for his good-nature, he is nevertheless a hard worker at whatever he undertakes, and if he sometimes shows a suspicious disposition it is only because his good-nature has been frequently imposed on.

When the last pencil had stopped scratching Joe gathered the slips together and after a moment's figuring announced that Steve had been elected Number One without a dissenting vote, that he himself had been made Number Two and that Phil was Number Three. If Perry felt disappointment he hid it, and when Phil declared that in his opinion Perry should have been elected instead of him, since Perry was, so to say, a charter member, Perry promptly disclaimed any desire of the sort.

"No, thanks," he said. "If I was secretary I'd have to keep the accounts and all that sort of thing, and I'm no good at it. You're the very fellow for the job, Phil."

The assemblage broke up shortly after, to meet again that evening at eight, Steve undertaking to have a map on hand then so that they might plan their cruise. As none of the seven was bound to secrecy, what happened is only what might have been expected. By the time the ball game was half over Steve and Joe had received enough applications for membership in the Adventure Club to have, in Joe's words, filled an ocean liner. It is probable that a large proportion of the applicants could not have obtained permission to join the expedition, but they were each and all terribly enthusiastic and eager to join, and it required all of Steve's and Joe's diplomacy to turn them away without hurting their feelings. Wink Wheeler - his real name was Warren, but no one ever called him that - refused politely but firmly to take no for an answer. Wink said he didn't care where he bunked and that he never ate anything on a boat, anyway, because he was always too seasick to bother about meals.

"One more won't matter, Steve," Wink pleaded. "Be a good chap and let me in, won't you? My folks are going out to California this Summer and I don't want to go, and they'll let me do anything I like. Tell you what, Steve. If you'll take me I'll buy something for the boat. I'll make the club a present of - of a tender or an anchor or whatever you say!"

Steve found it especially hard to turn Wink down, because he liked the fellow, just as everyone else did. Wink was eighteen and had been five years getting through school, but he was a big, good-hearted, jovial boy, and, as Steve reflected, one who would be a desirable companion on such an adventure as had been planned. Steve at last told Wink that he would speak to the others about him that evening, but that Wink was not to get his hopes up, and Wink took himself off whistling cheerfully and quite satisfied. But when Steve tentatively broached the matter of including one more member in the person of Wink Wheeler, Joe staggered him by announcing that he had promised Harry Corwin to intercede for the latter.

"He pestered the life out of me," explained Joe ruefully, "and I finally told him I'd ask you fellows. But I suppose we can't take two more. Nine would - um - be rather overdoing it, eh?"

Everyone agreed that it would. Han suggested that Wink Wheeler and Harry Corwin might toss up for the privilege of joining the club. "After all," he added, "we aren't all of us certain that we can go. If one or two of us drop out there'll be room for Wink and Harry, too."

"Seems to me," said Phil Street, "it might be a good plan to enlarge the membership to, say, twelve, and let the new members find a boat of their own. I dare say they could. Then -"

"Fine!" exclaimed Joe. "Harry and his brother have some sort of a motor-boat. He told me so today. That's a bully idea, Phil! With twelve of us we could divide up between the two boats -"

"How many will Corwin's boat hold?" asked Neil.

"I don't know. I'll see him and find out. But it ought to be big enough to hold four, anyway. There are seven of us now, and Wink and Harry and his brother Tom would make ten, and we could easily pick out two more."

"Let's make the membership thirteen," said Perry.

"Thirteen!" echoed Han. "Gee, that's unlucky!"

"Rot! Why, you've got thirteen letters in your name. George Hanford." Perry counted on his fingers. "This is the Adventure Club, isn't it? Well, starting out with thirteen members is an adventure right at the start!"

"Sure!" agreed Ossie. "Let's take a chance. It's only a silly what-do-you-call-it anyway."

"Meaning superstition?" asked Steve. "Well, I'm agreeable. Who else do we want? Bert Alley asked to join, and so did George Browne."

"And Casper Temple," added Joe. "And they're all good fellows. But I want it distinctly understood that I'm going on the *Cockatoo*."

"Me too!" exclaimed Perry. "All of us fellows must go on the *Cockatoo*. We were the first."

"But suppose Corwin's boat won't hold five?" said Han.

"We can squeeze eight into the *Cockatoo*, if we have to," said Steve. "Joe, you cut along and find Corwin and bring him up here. We might as well settle the thing now."

"All right, but don't settle about the cruise while I'm gone," answered Joe. "I'll have him here in ten minutes."

When the meeting adjourned that evening the club had added six new members and enlarged its fleet by the addition of the cabin-cruiser, *Follow Me*. It was just half-past ten when Joe and Steve produced the last of their supply of ginger-ale from under the window-seat and, utilising glasses, tooth-mugs and pewter trophies, the members present drank success to the Adventure Club.

CHAPTER III

CAST OFF!

Some two weeks later, or, to be exact, sixteen days, making the date therefor, the eighth day of July, a round-faced, freckle-cheeked youth in a pair of khaki trousers, white rubber-soled shoes, a light flannel shirt that had once been brown and was now the colour of much diluted coffee and a white duck hat sat on the forward deck of a trim motor-boat with his feet suspended above the untidy water of a slip. By turning his head slightly he could have looked across the sunlit surface of Buttermilk Channel to the green slopes of Governor's Island and, beyond the gleaming Statue of Liberty. But Perry Bush was far more interested in the approach that led from the noisy, granite-paved street behind a distant fence to the pier against which the boat was nestled. As he watched he sniffed gratefully of the mingled odours that came to him; the smell of salt water, of pitch and oakum, of paint from a neighbouring craft receiving her Summer dress, of fresh shavings and sawdust from the nearby shed whence came also the shriek of the band-saw and the *tap-tap* of mallets. Ballinger's Yacht Basin was a busy place at this time of the year, and the slips were crowded with sailboats and motor-boats, while many craft still stood, stilted and canvas-wrapped, in the shade of the long sheds. Perry whistled a gay tune softly as he basked there in the warm sunlight and awaited the arrival of the rest of the boat's crew.

Much had happened since that Thursday when they had toasted the Adventure Club in Steve's and Joe's room in Sumner. Graduation Day had sent them scurrying homeward.

Then had followed much correspondence with Steve. After an anxious four days, Perry and the rest had each received a brief but highly satisfactory telegram: "*Cockatoo* ours for two months. Meet Ballinger's Basin, Brooklyn, fourth." But work on the cruiser had delayed the starting date, and they had now been kicking their heels about New York for four days. Perry and Phil Street had been taken care of by Steve, and Joe had had Neil, Han and Ossie as his guests. At Bay Shore, on the south side of Long Island, the *Follow Me* was awaiting them impatiently. The *Follow Me* had been ready to put to sea for a full week.

Although Steve and Joe had provisioned the *Cockatoo* - which, by the way, was no longer the *Cockatoo*, but the *Adventurer*, having been renamed during the process of painting - the crew had not been altogether idle during their wait. Each had thought of something further to add. Ossie, who, as a special favour, was to be allowed to try his hand at cooking, had made several trips between a big department store on Fulton Street and had returned to the basin laden each time with mysterious packages, many of which rattled or clinked when deposited in the galley. Perry had purchased an inexpensive talking machine and a dozen records. Neil had contributed a patent life-preserver that looked like a waistcoat to be used by an Arctic explorer and was guaranteed to keep Barnum and Bailey's fat man afloat. Phil had supplied the cabin with magazines, few of them, to Perry's chagrin, of the sort anyone but a "highbrow" would care to tackle. Joe, as an after-thought, had stocked up heavily with Mother Somebody's Cure for Seasickness. George Hanford had tried to smuggle on board a black and white puppy about a foot long which he had bought on a street corner for two dollars and a half. Steve, however, had objected strenuously and Han had been forced to see the puppy's former owner and sell his purchase back for a dollar, the value of it having decreased surprisingly in a few hours. Even Steve had supplemented the boat's contents the day before by stowing two desperate-looking revolvers and several boxes of cartridges in a locker in the forward cabin.

Then, too, they had each outfitted more or less elaborately, according to their pocket-books. Steve and Joe had pointed out that, with seven aboard, locker room would be at a premium, and had urged the others to take as little in the way of personal luggage as they could get along with. But when the out-of-town boys got into the stores the advice was soon forgotten. Neil had outfitted as if he was about to set forth on a voyage around the world, and Han was not far behind him. Perry would have liked, too, to become the proud possessor of some of the things the former fellows brought aboard, but Perry's finances were low after he had paid for that talking machine, and so, with the exception of a new grey sweater, he had made no additions to his wardrobe. This morning he had volunteered to go to the basin early and superintend the loading of ice and water, and now, those things aboard, he was wondering, a trifle resentfully, why the others didn't come. They were to cast off at eleven and it was now well after ten.

"Probably," he muttered, edging back so that he could have the support of the big, round smoke-stack, "Neil's buying another necktie! It would serve them right if I started the thing up and went off without them." As, however, Perry knew absolutely nothing about a gasoline engine, there was little likelihood of his carrying that threat into action. In any case, there would have been no excuse, for less than a minute later he descried the tardy ones skirting the shed and coming along the wharf. They looked, Perry thought with satisfaction, very hot and disgruntled as, each carrying his belongings in a parcel so that there would be no bags to stow away, they approached the boat. Although Perry was no mechanician, he quite understood the operation of an electric horn, and now, swinging nimbly down to the bridge deck, he set the palm of his hand against a big black button. The result was all that he desired. An amazing, ear-splitting shriek broke the ordinary clamour of the scene. Perry smiled ecstatically and peered out and up from under the awning. But the half-dozen countenances that looked down at him expressed only disgust, and Joe's voice came to him even above the blast of the horn.

"Don't be a silly fool, Perry!" shouted Joe peevishly. "Let that alone and catch these bundles!"

Perry obeyed and one by one the fellows scrambled from wharf to boat. And, having reached the bridge deck, they subsided exhaustedly onto the two cushioned seats or the gunwale. Perry viewed their inflamed, perspiring faces in smiling surprise. "What did you do?" he asked. "Run all the way?"

"Joe got us on the wrong car," panted Neil, "and we went halfway to Coney Island, I guess."

"It wasn't my fault any more than it was yours," growled Joe. "You had eyes, hadn't you?"

"We had eyes," replied Ossie from behind his handkerchief, as he wiped his streaming face, "but we aren't supposed to know where these silly cars go to."

"I didn't have any trouble," murmured Perry.

"Well, we did," said Han resentfully. "We waited ten minutes on a broiling-hot corner and then, when we did get another car, it got blocked behind ten thousand drays and we had to foot it about eleven miles! Got any ice-water aboard?"

"We've got ice and we've got water," replied Perry. "If you mix 'em in the proper proportions -"

"Oh, dry up and blow away," muttered Han, dragging himself painfully down the companion on his way to the galley. Phil Street smiled.

"Seems to me we're starting our adventure rather inauspiciously," he said. "If we have a grouch before we leave the dock what's going to happen later?"

"Maybe it's a good thing to have it now and get over it," laughed Steve. "It was hot, though! And it isn't much cooler here. Let's get under way, fellows, and find a breeze. It will take us the better part of four hours to get to Bay Shore, anyway, and I telephoned Wink yesterday that we'd be there by three. Every fellow into sea-togs as quick as he can make it. Joe and Phil and I bunk aft, the rest of you in the main cabin. Get your things put away neatly, fellows. Anyone caught being disorderly will be keel-hauled. Have a look at this thermometer, Joe. It's almost eighty-nine! Let's get out of here in a hurry!"

For the next ten minutes the fellows busied themselves as Steve had directed. All, that is, save Perry. As Perry was already dressed for sea he used his leisure to sit in the hatchway of the after cabin and converse entertainingly with the occupants until, on the score that he was keeping the air out, he was driven up to the cockpit. There he perched himself in one of the four comfortable wicker chairs, placed his feet on the leather-cushioned seat across the stern and languorously observed a less fortunate person scrape the deck of a sloop on the far side of the slip.

Suppose that, while the *Adventurer's* crew prepares for service, we have a look over the boat. The *Adventurer*, late the *Cockatoo*, was a forty-foot V-bottom, military type cruiser, with a nine-foot beam and a draught of two feet and six inches. Below the water-line she was painted a dark green. Above it she was freshly, immaculately white as to hull, while decks and smoke-stack were buff. The exterior bulkheads were of panelled mahogany, and a narrow strip of mahogany edged the deck. There was a refreshing lack of gold in sight, and, viewed from alongside, the *Adventurer* had a very business-like appearance. As she was of the raised-deck cabin type, with full head-room everywhere, she stood well above the water, and the low, sweeping lines that suggest speed were lacking. But the *Adventurer* had speed, nevertheless, for under the bridge deck was a six-cylinder 6x6 Van Lyte engine that could send her along at twenty miles an hour when necessary. On the stern was the legend "ADVENTURER: NEW YORK," and the name appeared again on each of the mahogany boards that housed the sidelights. The cockpit, which was self-bailing, was roomy enough to accommodate seven persons comfortably. A broad leather-cushioned seat ran across the stern and there were four wicker chairs besides. Life preservers were ingeniously strapped under the chair seats and two others hung at each side of the after cabin door.

The after cabin, or owner's stateroom, held two extension seats which at night were converted into wide and comfortable berths. At the forward end a lavatory occupied one side and a clothes locker the other. Other lockers occupied the space between the seats and the three ports. This compartment, like the main cabin, was enamelled in cream-white with mahogany trim. Three steps led to the bridge deck, a roomy place which housed engine, steering wheel and all controls. The engine, although under deck, was readily accessible by means of sectional hatches. On the steering column were wheel, self-starter switch, spark, throttle and clutch, making it easily possible for one person to operate the boat if necessary. Two seats were built against the after bulkhead, chart boxes flanked the forward hatchway and the binnacle was above the steering column. Forward, the compartment was glassed in, but on other sides khaki curtains were depended on in bad weather. When not in use the curtains rolled up to the edge of the awning, which was set on a pipe-frame.

From the bridge deck three steps led down to the main cabin. Here in the daytime were two longitudinal couches with high upholstered backs. At night the backs swung out and up to form berths, so that the compartment supplied sleeping accomodations for four persons. There were roomy lockers under the seats and at meal times an extension table made a miraculous appearance and seated eight. Forward of the main cabin was the galley, gleaming with white enamel and brass. It was fitted with a large ice-chest, many lockers, a sink with running water, a two-burner alcohol stove with oven and a multitude of plate-racks. It was the lightest place in the boat, for, besides a light-port on each side, it had as well a hatch overhead. The hatch, although water-tight, was made to open for the admission of ice and supplies. Still forward, in the nose of the boat, was a large water tank and, beyond that, the rope locker. The gasoline tanks, of which there were four, held two hundred and fifty gallons. The boat was lighted by electricity in all parts by means of a generator and storage battery. An eight-foot tender rested on chocks atop the main cabin. The boat carried no signal mast, but flag-poles at bow and stern and abaft the bridge deck frame held the Union Jack, the yacht ensign and the club burgee. All in all, the *Adventurer* was a smart and finely appointed craft, and a capable one, too. Steve's father had had her built only a little more than a year ago and she had seen but scant service. In the inelegant but expressive phraseology of Perry, "she was a rip-snorting corker of a boat." The consensus of opinion was to the effect that Mr. Chapman was "a peach to let them have it," and there was an unuttered impression that that kind-hearted gentleman was taking awful chances!

For, after all, except that Steve had had a brief week or so on the boat the preceding Summer and that Joe had taken two days of instruction in gasoline engine operation, not a member of the crew knew much of the work ahead. Still, George Hanford had operated a twelve-foot motor dingey at one time, Phil Street had sailed a knockabout and all had an average amount of common-sense, and it seemed that, with luck, they might somehow manage to escape death by drowning! Mr. Chapman surely must have had a good deal of faith in Steve and his companions or he would never have consented to their operating the cruiser without the aid of a seasoned navigator. As for the boys themselves, they anticipated many difficulties and some hazards, but, with the confidence of youth, they expected to "muddle through," and, as Neil said, what they didn't know now they soon would.

At exactly seven minutes past eleven by the ship's clock the *Adventurer* gave a prolonged screech and, moorings cast off, edged her way out of the basin and dipped her nose in the laughing waters of the bay, embarked at last on a voyage that was destined to fully vindicate her new name.

CHAPTER IV

THE *FOLLOW ME*

Two days before they had decided that Steve was to be captain, Joe, chief engineer, Phil, first mate, Perry, second mate, Ossie, steward, Neil, cabin boy and Han, crew. Neil and Han had naturally rebelled at being left without office or title and the omission had been laughingly remedied to their entire satisfaction. In fact, Han was quite stuck up over his official position, pointing out that it might be possible for a boat to get along without a captain or mate or even a steward, but that a crew was absolutely essential. He declared his intention of purchasing a yachting cap at the first port of call and having the inscription "Crew" worked on it in gold bullion.

When the *Adventurer* left her berth each member of the boat's company was at his post, or, at least, at what he surmised to be his post. Steve, of course, was at the control, Joe, with the hatches up, was watching his engine approvingly, Phil, boathook in hand, was on the forward deck, Perry hovered around Steve, begging to be allowed to blow the whistle, Ossie and Neil watched from opposite sides of the bridge deck and Han, in the role of crew, hitched his trousers at intervals, touched his cap when anyone so much as looked at him and said "Ay, ay, sir!" at the slightest provocation. And with all hands on duty the cruiser pointed her white bow towards The Narrows.

Steve never took his eyes from the course for more than a moment until they had passed Coney Island Light, for there were many craft bustling or slopping about and it really required some navigation to get through The Narrows and

RALPH HENRY BARBOUR

past Gravesend Bay without running into something. Perry suspected that Steve was working the whistle overtime, but realized that too many precautions were better than too few. It was Perry's ambition to learn navigation so that he might ultimately be entrusted with the wheel, and to that end he stood at Steve's elbow until, when they gained the Main Channel, Ossie's dulcet voice was heard proclaiming, "Grub, fellows!" from below. Steve was rather too preoccupied to be very informative, but Perry did manage to imbibe some information. For instance, he learned that a sailing craft had the right of way over a power craft, something he had not known previously, and observed that a large proportion of them used that right to its limit. He got quite incensed with a small, blunt-nosed schooner which insisted on crossing the *Adventurer's* course just as they were passing Fort Hamilton. Steve had to slow down rather hurriedly to avoid a collision and Perry viewed the two occupants of the schooner's deck with a scowl as they lazed across the cruiser's bows.

"Cheeky beggars," he muttered.

He also learned the whistle code that morning: one blast for starboard, two for port, four short blasts for danger and three for going astern. Joe, who had applied oil to every part of the engine that he could reach, supplied the added information that a sailboat under way on the starboard tack had the right of way over anything afloat - with the possible exception of a torpedo! - and that other craft had to turn to port in passing them. Joe had wrested that bit of knowledge from a volume entitled, "Motor Boats and Boating," which he carried in a side pocket every minute of the trip, and passed it on with evident pride. For the next few days he discovered other interesting items in that precious book and divulged them at intervals with what to Perry seemed a most offensive assumption of superiority.

"You just read that in your old book," Perry would grumble. "Anybody could do that!" Nevertheless, he hearkened and remembered against the time when the conduct of the boat should be handed over to the hands of the efficient second mate. When Joe became insufferably informative Perry blandly asked him questions about the engine, such as, "What's the difference, Joe, between a two-cycle and a four-cycle motor?" or "What happens when the water-jacket becomes unbuttoned?" and was delighted to find that Joe lapsed into silence until he had had time to surreptitiously consult his book.

Today, however, Joe's ignorance of motors mattered not at all, for the engine ran sweetly and the *Adventurer* churned through the green water without a falter. More than once Joe might have been observed gazing down at the six cylinder-heads surmounted by their maze of wires with an expression of awe. Joe's thoughts probably might have been put into words thus: "Yes, I see you doing it, but - but *why?*"

Steve didn't go down to the cabin for dinner, but ate it as best he could on the bridge. Neil, in his capacity of cabin-boy, arranged a folding stool beside him, and from that, at intervals between moving the wheel, blowing the whistle or anxiously scanning the course, Steve seized his food. The others descended to the main cabin and squeezed themselves about the table, which, adorned with a cloth of wonderful sheen and whiteness that bore the cruiser's former name and flag woven in the centre, held a plentiful supply of canned beans, fried bacon, potato chips, bread and butter and raspberry jam. Everything was thrillingly fine, from the pure linen tablecloth and napkins to the silverware. The plates held the same design that was worked into the napery, as did even the knives and forks and spoons. Ossie was apologetic as to the menu, although he need not have been.

"There wasn't time to do much cooking," he said, "and, besides, I haven't got the hang of things yet. I never tried to do anything on an alcohol stove before. It takes longer, seems to me. I couldn't get the oven heated until about five minutes ago, and so if those potato-chips aren't very warm -"

"I'm warm enough, if they aren't," said Neil. "How do you

open these little round window things?"

"Turn the thumb-screws," advised Han. "I think everything's bully, and I'm as hungry as a bear. Pass the beans, Perry. Got any more tea out there, cook?"

"Yes, but I'm steward and not cook," replied Ossie, arising from his camp-stool and stepping into the galley. "Hand over the bread plate, someone, and I'll cut some more. Bet you it's going to cost us something for grub, fellows!"

"Well," responded Han, "I'd rather go broke that way than some others. What kind of tea is this, Ossie?"

"Ceylon. Doesn't it suit you?"

"Oh, I can worry it down, thanks. Sugar, please, Phil. I generally drink orange pekoe, though. You might lay in a few pounds of it at the next stop."

"I might," said Ossie, resuming his place at the end of the board, "and then again I might not. And the probabilities are not. If you don't want all the potatoes, Joe, you may shove them along this way."

The repast was frequently interrupted by the shrill blast of the whistle, and whenever that sounded most of the diners scrambled up to peer interestedly through the ports. In fact, so loth were they to miss anything that might be happening that they finished dinner in record time, consuming dessert, which consisted of bananas and pears, outside. Ossie alone remained below, and from the galley came the clatter of dishes and a cheerful tune as the steward cleared away and washed up. Joe smiled at Phil.

"Ossie's having the time of his life now," he said, "but wait until the novelty wears off. Then we'll hear some tall kicking about the dishwashing, or I miss my guess."

"We'll have to take turns helping him at that," said Steve. "If we don't he's likely to mutiny. There's Coney over there, fellows."

The others gathered on the port side to gaze across the water at the crowded beach and the colourful maze of buildings. "It looks jolly, doesn't it?" asked Han. "Couldn't we run in closer, Steve?"

"We could, but it would take us out of our course. I'm heading for Rockaway Point over there. We've got a good ways to go yet before we reach Fire Island." Steve had the chart opened before him and he laid a finger on the point mentioned.

"Looks like it would be more fun to duck in there," said Neil, vaguely indicating the neighbourhood of Hempstead Bay.

"Maybe it would," answered the Captain, "but there are too many islands and things to suit me. I'd rather stay outside here and slip in through Fire Island Inlet. After I get used to running this hooker I'll take her anywhere there's a heavy dew, but right now I'm all for the open sea, Neil."

Phil and Han, who had never before gazed on the marvels of Coney Island, even from a distance, were listening to Joe's tales of the delights of that entrancing resort and following his finger as he pointed out the features he recognised. "There's the coaster where I bounced up and came down on a nail," he chuckled. "It was a fine, able-bodied nail, too, and I - um - had to stay on it all the rest of the trip because the car was so crowded there wasn't room to shift."

"Smell the peanuts, fellows," murmured Perry dreamily. "Gee, I wish I had some!"

Ossie appeared on deck ten minutes later and was very indignant because he had not been informed that they were passing Coney. "I think some of you lobsters might have sung out," he mourned. "I've never seen Coney Island."

"Well, have a look," laughed Han. "That's it back there."

"Huh! Can't see anything at this distance," growled Ossie. "It's just a smear of buildings. What's the place ahead there!"

"Rockaway," answered Joe, "and that's Jamaica Bay in there. Say, there's some sea on, isn't there?"

In fact the *Adventurer* was now doing a good deal of plunging as she made her way through the long swells that swept around the sandy point. And she wasn't satisfied with merely kicking her head and heels up, either, for with the forward and aft motion there was considerable rocking, and as the point came abreast a shower of spray deluged the forward deck and spattered in on the bridge. At Steve's direction the windows were closed, Han performing the task with many "Ay, ay, sirs!" Joe looked anxious and presently sought the forward cabin, reappearing a minute later to ask all and sundry if they knew where he had put his supply of "anti-seasick stuff." No one could tell him and he again took himself off, and before he could locate the medicine the *Adventurer* had passed the inlet and had settled down on an even keel again. Han and Ossie spread themselves out on the forward cabin roof and the others made themselves comfortable on the seats of the bridge deck, Phil pointing out seriously and with evident satisfaction that the cushions were not only cushions but life-preservers as well. Perry was for borrowing Phil's fountain-pen and putting his name on one.

There was no longer any talk of being too warm, for the breeze was straight from the southeast and soon sent them, one after another, into the cabins for their sweaters. They passed Rockaway Beach a good three miles to port and by half-past one were off Point Lookout. Every instant held interest, for many pleasure boats were out and their white sails gleamed in the crisp sunlight. Three porpoise appeared off Short Beach and proved very companionable, for they stayed with the *Adventurer* for quite ten minutes. One placed himself directly in front of the boat and the others took up positions about six feet apart on the starboard bow, and for two miles or more they maintained their stations, their dusky, gleaming backs arching from the water with the regularity of clock-work. Most of the boys had never seen the fish before and were much interested. Joe called them "puffing pigs" and Perry insisted that they were dolphins, and a fervid argument followed. They finally agreed, at Phil's suggestion, to compromise and call them "porphins." Possibly the discussion bored the subjects, or maybe they were insulted by the title applied to them, for about the time Joe and Perry reached an agreement the porpoise disappeared as suddenly as they had arrived on the scene and it was minutes later before the puzzled mariners descried them heading shoreward some distance away.

They missed Ossie after that and when he was found he was stretched out on a seat in the main cabin sound asleep and snoring. Neil came back with the news that one of the "puffing pigs" had flopped aboard and was asleep below. Steve took advantage of plain sailing to instruct Joe, Phil and Perry in the handling of the wheel and controls, and each of the pupils took his turn at guiding the cruiser along the sandy coast. Fire Island Inlet was reached shortly before three and Steve took the wheel again and ran the *Adventurer* past Jack's Island, around the curve of Short Beach and into the waters of the Great South Bay. There was still a six-mile run to their anchorage, however, and it was nearly four when the cruiser at last crept in among the clustered craft off Bay Shore and dropped her anchor. A hundred yards away a cluster of boys on the deck of a sturdy cabin-cruiser swung their caps and sent a hail across. Steve seized the megaphone from its rack and answered.

"*Follow Me*, ahoy!" he shouted.

"Ahoy yourself!" was the ribald reply. "We're coming over!"

The crew of the *Follow Me* tumbled into a tiny dingey, cast off and were lost to sight beyond the intervening craft. Then they reappeared, their small boat so deep that the water almost spilled over the sides, Wink Wheeler struggling with a pair of ludicrously short oars and the other five laughingly urging him on.

"Throw a couple of fenders over, Han," instructed Steve, "and stand by with your boat-hook."

The *Follow Me's* tender crept alongside amidst noisy greetings, Perry performing excruciatingly on the whistle until pulled away, and in another moment the visitors were aboard. They were a nice-looking, upstanding lot, already well sunburned by a week afloat. Wink Wheeler was the oldest of the six, for he was eighteen. Harry Corwin, Bert Alley and Caspar Temple were seventeen and George Browne, or "Brownie," as he was called, and Tom Corwin were sixteen. First of all they had to see the boat and so the whole gathering trooped from one end to the other, exclaiming and admiring.

"The *Follow Me's* a regular tub compared with this palace," said Harry Corwin. "Why, there isn't anything finer than this along the South Shore, I guess!"

"Don't you call our boat names," protested "Brownie." "The *Follow Me* may not be as nifty as this, but she's one fine little boat, just the same. How long did it take you to come from New York, Joe?"

"Nearly four hours and a half, but we ran slow. I guess we could have done it in three hours easily if we'd tried to. This boat can do twenty at a pinch. How fast is the *Follow Me?*"

"She's done eighteen," answered Harry Corwin, "but fourteen's her average gait. She burns up gas like the dickens when she does any more. Yesterday we went to Freeport in fifty-seven minutes, and that's a good seventeen and a half miles. She had to hump herself, though."

After the wonders of the *Adventurer* had been exhausted the boys gathered on the bridge deck and Steve laid a chart on the floor and they discussed their plans. It had already been decided that they should cruise northward as far as Maine. As there was no hurry in getting there, they were to take things easy, stopping at such points as promised interest and putting into harbour at night. As it was already after four o'clock, they finally concluded to stay where they were until morning, although the *Follow Me* crowd were eager to be away. "Our first harbour would be Ponquogue," said Steve, "and that's a good forty-six or-seven mile run. Personally, I don't care much about messing around outside after dark. This is all new water to me. If we start in the morning we'll have plenty of time to run as far as Shelter Island, if we want to."

This was agreed to, although Perry protested that as the charts showed a life-saving station every five miles or so all down the shore it was a shame not to take a chance. "I've always wanted to be taken off a sinking ship in a breeches-buoy," he said.

"Would you mind being wrecked in the daytime?" asked Neil. "I'd love to see you in a breeches-buoy, Perry, and I couldn't if it was dark."

"Let's all go up to the hotel for dinner," suggested Wink Wheeler. "They have dandy feeds there, and maybe we can scare up some fun. Any of you fellows like to bowl?"

"First of all," said Han, "we want to see your boat, fellows. Let's go over now. I'm ready for hotel grub if the rest of you are. Can we all go, Steve, or does someone have to stay behind and look after the boat?"

"That's the crew's duty," said Phil gravely. "We'll bring you back a sandwich, Han."

"Yes, a Han-sandwich," added Perry.

When he had been toppled backward down the after cabin steps Harry Corwin said that they'd been in the habit of leaving the *Follow Me* unguarded for hours at a time and that so far no one had molested her, and Steve decided that it would be safe enough if they locked the cabins. So presently the *Adventurer's* tender was lifted off the chocks and put overboard and after hasty toilets the boys piled into it and the two dingeys, each loaded to the limit, set off for the *Follow Me*. The latter was a thirty-four foot craft, with a hunting cabin that reached almost to the stern, leaving a cockpit scarcely large enough to swing a cat in; although, as Perry remarked, it wasn't likely anyone would want to swing a cat there. The cabin was surprisingly roomy and held four berths, while a fifth bunk was placed forward of the tiny galley. The latter was intended for the crew but at present it was the quarters of "Brownie." The sixth member of the ship's company occupied at night a mattress placed on the floor and philosophically explained that sleeping there had the advantage of security; there was no chance to roll out of bed in rough weather. The engine compartment lay between cabin and cockpit and held a six-cylinder engine. Steering was done from the cockpit, under shelter of an awning, but the engine control was below. The *Follow Me* was four years old and had seen much service, but she had been newly painted, varnished and overhauled and looked like a thoroughly comfortable and seaworthy boat. She was copper painted below the water-line and black above, with a gilt line and her name in gilt on bows and stern. Compared to the *Adventurer* she was a modest enough craft, but her six mariners asked nothing better and secretly believed that in rough weather she would put the bigger boat to shame. Captain Corwin levied on the slender supply of ginger-ale and sarsaparilla contained in the tiny ice-chest and after that they again set forth, this time for the nearest landing.

They "did" the town exhaustively and at six-thirty descended on the hotel thirteen strong and demanded to be placed together at one table. It is doubtful if the hotel management made much money on the thirteen dinners served to the boys, for everyone of them ate as though he hadn't seen food for days. Somewhere around eight or half-past they dragged themselves back to the boats and paddled out to the *Adventurer*, where, since the evening was decidedly chilly, they thronged the after cabin and flowed out into the cockpit. Perry started up his talking machine and played his dozen records over a number of times, and everyone talked at once - except some who sang - and, in the words of the country newspapers, "a pleasant time was had by all." And at ten the *Follow Me's* crew got back into their dingey and went off into the darkness of a starlight night, rather noisy still in a sleepy way, and, presumably, reached their destination. At least, no more was heard of them that night. On the *Adventurer* berths were pulled out or let down and a quarter of an hour after the departure of the visitors not a sound was to be heard save the lapping of the water against the hull and the peaceful breathing of seven healthily tired boys.

RALPH HENRY BARBOUR

CHAPTER V

SUNDAY ASHORE

Before the sun had much more than climbed to a position where it could peer over the low yellow ridge of Fire Island and see what the Adventure Club was up to, the two cruisers were chug-chugging out of the harbour with all flags flying. First went the *Adventurer*, as flag-ship of the fleet, to use Neil's metaphor, and, a little way behind came the *Follow Me*, her black hull and battleship-grey deck reminding the occupants of the other boat of one of the "puffing pigs" of yesterday. The bay was almost as smooth as the proverbial mill-pond this morning, and the slanting shafts of sunlight cast strange and beautiful shades of gold and copper on the tiny wavelets. It was still cool, and in the shadow of the bridge deck one felt a bit shivery. But the sun promised a warm day. The crew was polishing bright-work rather awkwardly but most industriously and with a fine willingness, explaining that if he polished brass some other poor Indian would have to swab decks, a remark which inspired Neil to state with much emphasis that cleaning decks was not, at all events, within the province of the ship's boy, and that, anyway, he had helped with the dishes and that right now he was going to lie in the sun on the galley roof and that if anyone disturbed him there'd be trouble.

Joe had been having a fine time with his engine. He was getting on terms of real familiarity with it now, having lost some of the awe with which he had regarded it yesterday. Today he called it "She" almost patronisingly and even dared lay his hand on the cylinders with a knowing cock of his head. Perry, looking on, asked sarcastically if he was feeling the engine's pulse, and Joe haughtily replied that he wanted to make sure the cylinders weren't overheating. Ossie, emerging from the cabin, wiping his hands on his khaki trousers after wringing out his dish cloths, gave it as his opinion that if there was any overeating done it would not be done by the engine, accompanying the statement with a meaning glance at Perry.

About this time the *Follow Me* left her position astern and began to creep alongside. Steve supposed she wanted to send a message across and told the others on the deck to keep still a minute. But the *Follow Me* kept on her way, the fellows sprawling around her deck and cockpit looking across the few fathoms of water in silence.

"Well, what do you know about that?" gasped Neil. "She's trying to pass us!"

Steve grunted, smiled and advanced his throttle. The click-click from under the engine hatches became hurried and louder. Joe wrinkled his forehead anxiously. The *Adventurer* stopped going astern of the other boat and for a little distance they hung bow to bow. They saw Harry Corwin, at the wheel of the *Follow Me*, lower his head to speak to his brother in the engine room. The *Follow Me* began to forge ahead again, slowly but certainly.

"Give her more gas, Steve," begged Perry. "We can't have a little old 'puffing pig' of a boat like that walking away from us. Look at those idiots grin!"

"And watch them change their faces," laughed Steve as he drew the throttle forward another two or three notches. Under the hatches the engine uttered a new note and a quick jarring became felt. Joe's anxiety increased to uneasiness.

"Say, Steve, do you think - is it all right - I mean -"

"She's only doing about seventeen," replied Steve calmly. "The throttle isn't nearly open yet. But I guess that's enough," he added as he glanced across the water. Perry, leaning across the gunwale, beckoned insultingly.

"Come on!" he called. "What are you stopping there for?"

The *Follow Me* replied to the taunt, but what the reply was they didn't know on the *Adventurer*, for the latter was ahead now by its full length and gaining perceptibly every moment. Tom Corwin's head appeared over the cabin roof, he took a look at the rival craft and popped from sight again. The *Follow Me* stopped going back and hung with her nose abreast the *Adventurer's* stern. Phil, who had been writing a letter in the cabin, emerged and joined the group outside.

"How fast is she going, Steve?" he asked.

"About seventeen, I think. Still, Harry said the *Follow Me's* best was eighteen, and she isn't losing any, and so we may be doing eighteen, too. Guess we might as well settle the matter right now, though."

With which he pulled the throttle to the limit, and the white cruiser, quivering from stem to stern, forged ahead. "We're doing a good twenty miles an hour now," shouted Steve above the hum of the motor, "and she won't go any faster unless we get out and push!"

But twenty miles was fast enough to distance the *Follow Me*, although that boat held on gamely all the way across the bay and only slowed down when, a good quarter of a mile behind the *Adventurer*, she was abreast Pelican Bar. The *Adventurer* dropped her gait to twelve and presently the black cruiser, having negotiated the inlet in the wake of the other craft, drew within hailing distance and Harry Corwin called across through the megaphone.

"Some boat, Steve!" he shouted. "We're satisfied!"

Steve waved back and the two cruisers settled down to their

forty-mile run along the shore, the *Follow Me* gliding smoothly along abaft the *Adventurer's* starboard beam. They sighted few other craft this morning, and, as there was a deal of sameness in the coast, the fellows settled down to various occupations. Steve conducted a second class in navigation, with Perry and Han as pupils, and Perry was allowed to take the wheel all the way from Smith's Point to a position off the Moriches Life-Saving Station. Phil went on with his letters, Ossie performed mysterious rites in the galley, with Han looking on interestedly from atop the dish-board, and Neil, exhausted by his labours as crew, reclined on the seat in the cockpit and stared sleepily at a blue and unclouded sky. Joe hunched himself on a seat on the bridge deck and studied his book on motor boating, becoming, if truth were told, more and more mystified as to the working of that remarkable affair that was click-clicking away under his feet.

The *Adventurer* reached the inlet to Shinnecock Bay a few minutes past ten and, closely followed by her companion boat, put through and turned her nose past Ponquogue Point. As Comorant Point drew near the shores of the bay closed in and the cruiser turned to port and, signalling her way past various craft, finally came to a pause outside the canal entrance. When the *Follow Me* floated alongside Wink Wheeler called across.

"What do you say to going ashore, fellows?" he asked. "It looks like a jolly sort of place. We've got plenty of time, haven't we?"

"All the time in the world and nothing to do," replied Steve cheerfully. "We'll make that landing over there and you can come alongside us, Harry."

Ten minutes later they were stretching their legs ashore. Canoe Place held plenty to interest them. The view was magnificent, for on one side of them lay Shinnecock Bay, across whose still, pond-like waters they had just sailed, and on the other stretched the blue expanse of Great Peconic Bay, sun-bathed, aglint with rippling waves and dotted with white sails. A small boy with one suspender performing the duty of two and a straw hat minus about everything except the brim offered to guide them and his proposition was quickly accepted and a bright new quarter changed hands. The quaint old Inn was visited and their informant gravely pointed to two sentinel willow trees and told them that "them trees was planted by Napoleon a couple o' hunerd years ago. He got 'em some place called Saint Helen. They had him in prison there for somethin'." The boys viewed the willows doubtfully, but, as Phil said, it was more fun to believe the extraordinary tale and they tried hard to do so. Steve attempted to secure more historical information from the small boy, but the latter appeared to have exhausted his fund. After that they viewed several Summer estates from respectful distances and, finding that their guide had nothing further of real interest for them, went back to the landing and re-embarked.

A quarter-mile or so of artificial canal took them through the narrow neck of land between the two bays and let them out in a cove beyond whose mouth the waters of Great Peconic stretched, apparently illimitable. The course was set northeast by east and they began the trip to Shelter Island. About half an hour later Joe discovered that the *Follow Me* was far behind and it was soon evident that she had stopped. After a moment Steve decided to turn back and see what was wrong, and when the *Adventurer* rounded the smaller boat's stern they learned that the *Follow Me* was having engine trouble. For a few minutes the *Adventurer* hovered by, and then, as there was a fair breeze blowing now and Joe and Neil were showing interest in the sea-sickness remedy, Steve suggested a tow and Harry Corwin, after some hesitation, pocketed his pride and agreed. A little before one o'clock the two boats slipped into North Sea Harbour and dropped anchors. While the *Follow Me* doctored her engine the *Adventurer* sat down to a delayed dinner. Ossie gloomily predicted that everything would be spoiled, but if it was, no one save Ossie apparently knew it. There was broiled bluefish and boiled potatoes and spinach and sliced cucumbers that day, followed by a marvellous concoction which the steward called a prune pudding. Perry said he didn't care what it was called so long as it came, and, please he'd like some more! No cook can withstand such a compliment as that, and Ossie cast off his gloom. They all declared that that dinner was just about the best they had ever eaten, and they meant it, and Ossie swelled visibly with pride and almost declined Han's half-hearted offer to help wash dishes!

When the rest went back to the deck and saw the fellows on the *Follow Me* eating sandwiches and other items of a cold repast on deck they felt rather apologetic, and Joe and Steve slung the tender over and paddled across to lend what assistance they might. But they found Tom Corwin, very dirty and hot and somewhat peevish, reassembling the engine with the help of "Brownie," and learned that the trouble had been discovered and that the boat would go just as soon as they could get her together again, which, from present indications, would be some time the day after tomorrow! Harry Corwin told Steve he had better go ahead, that there was no use in the *Adventurer* lying around and waiting, but Steve replied that there was no hurry and that they'd stand by. The atmosphere on the *Follow Me* was not very cheerful and the visitors went back to their own craft after a decent lapse of time. About three the fellows donned swimming tights and went in from the boat and had a fine time in the water, and by the time they had had enough of that there came a heartening *chug-chug-chug* from the *Follow Me's* exhaust and Wink announced that they were ready to go on.

As a result of the delay, it was almost six when they reached Shelter Island and steered the cruiser to an anchorage. They had supper ashore at seven, having dressed themselves in shore-going attire, but it was noticeable that it was the *Follow Me's* company who made the most of the meal. Neil met up with an acquaintance on the hotel porch after supper - they chose to call it supper although it was really a full-course dinner - and that meeting led to introductions and the boys "did the society act," to use Perry's disgusted phrase, for the rest of the evening. As it was a Saturday night there was a dance going on, and Steve and Joe and Han, of the *Adventurer's* crowd, and several

RALPH HENRY BARBOUR

of the other boat's company, took part. They didn't get back to the boats until almost midnight, and Perry fell asleep in the dingey, on the second trip, and had to be practically hoisted aboard. He muttered protestingly until he had been dumped in his berth and then promptly went to sleep as he was.

They spent the next day at Shelter Island, not because anyone considered it wrong to cruise on Sunday, but because Steve and Joe and Han had discovered attractions at the hotel. Perry demanded that the question of staying be put to a vote and the rest agreed, but the result wasn't what Perry had hoped for because Neil basely cast his ballot with Steve and Joe and Han. The four went off soon after breakfast, having spent much time and effort on their various attires, and weren't seen again until late afternoon. At least, they weren't seen again aboard the cruiser until that time, although Perry, Phil and Ossie, following them ashore after dinner, were scandalised to see them strolling around quite brazenly in the company of an equal number of young ladies.

"Girls!" snorted Perry scornfully. "Why, the big chumps, they look as if they liked it! Gee, it's enough to sicken a fellow!"

CHAPTER VI

IN THE FOG

"We've been going two whole days now," declared Perry, "and we haven't even glimpsed an adventure." It was Tuesday morning and the two cruisers were lying side by side in New Bedford harbour. A light drizzle was falling and even under the awning of the bridge deck everything was coated with a film of moisture. The *Adventurer* and the *Follow Me* had done just short of a hundred miles yesterday, reaching the present port at nightfall. They had averaged fifteen miles an hour and neither engine had missed an explosion all day long. Joe had been rather stuck-up over the way his engine had performed and had been inclined to take a good share of the credit to himself. Perry, however, had declared that the only reason the thing had run was because Joe had left it alone.

"It's lucky for us you're afraid to touch it," said Perry. "If you weren't we'd have been wallowing around somewhere between here and Africa two days ago!"

It had been too late to go ashore for sight-seeing last evening, and they had put it off until morning. And now it was drizzling in a steady, whole-hearted way that promised to make sight-seeing a miserable business. Some of the crew of the *Follow Me* had come aboard to discuss plans and the question was whether to remain in harbour and await better weather or to set out again and run as far as Martha's Vineyard. Perry was all for action, and he had the support of numerous others, but Steve pointed out that running the cruiser in such weather in strange waters was not over pleasant. "It's all well enough for the rest of you, for all you have to do is lie around and read, but it's another thing to stand up there at the wheel and keep from running into the landscape!"

"Give her to me," advised Perry. "I'll get her to Edgartown or wherever you want to go, right-side-up with care."

"If you take the wheel," said Han, "I get out and walk every foot of the way."

"Better put your rubbers on," suggested Wink Wheeler.

"You fellows make me very tired," continued Perry severely. "You call yourselves the Adventure Club and start out to see some sport, and then the first time there's a heavy mist you want to stick around an old harbour for fear you'll get damp! We've been going two whole days now, and we haven't even glimpsed an adventure!"

"An adventure is one thing," said Ossie, "and getting drowned is something else again. Tell you what, Perry; if you are so keen for sport why don't you slip into the tender and run over to Vineyard Haven yourself? We'll follow along tomorrow, or maybe this afternoon."

"I want to see this town," said Joe. "There's lots to look at in here. Whaling ships and a museum and - and lots of romantic things."

"The whaling ships are all gone now," said Perry disdainfully. "They've chopped them all up and sold them by the cord for fire wood. I know, for we bought a lot of it once. It cost dad about ten dollars for express and didn't burn any different from any other wood. My grandmother -"

Steve groaned. "For the love of lemons, Perry, don't resurrect your grandmother. Let the poor old lady lie."

"She isn't dead," denied Perry indignantly. "She's ninety-one and a heap smarter than you are."

"Perry," charged Joe severely, "I distinctly remember you telling us that your grandmother died of sea-sickness."

"I didn't. I told you she ate lemons and -"

"Died of acid stomach? Oh, all right. I knew she was dead."

"Oh, dry up! She ate lemons to keep from being sea-sick, you idiot. And if you ate them you wouldn't have to lug around a lot of silly medicine that doesn't amount to a row of pins. And if -"

"All very interesting," interrupted Phil mildly, "but it isn't deciding whether we're to stay here or go on. Personally, I think that that should be up to the captain. If he isn't to decide whether the weather is right or wrong, who is?"

"That's so," agreed several. "Steve's the captain. What you say goes, Steve."

"Very well. Then we'll stay here until it stops misting, or, at any rate, until tomorrow. If it's still nasty then and you fellows want to go on, I'll go. Now let's go ashore and see what's doing."

"O Harry!" called Wink. "We're going to stay until tomorrow. Come ashore."

In spite of the drizzle they found a good deal to interest them in New Bedford, and Joe actually did find a whaler, although it was no longer in commission. At noon, Ossie, having made many purchases in the town, served a dinner that made the world look a lot brighter. Afterwards the crews of the two boats exchanged calls, read, dozed, played the graphophone and didn't much care whether it drizzled or not. Toward the end of the day the sun peered forth experimentally and there followed another expedition ashore. But the sun soon gave up its attempt to do any business that day and the drizzle set in harder than ever. In the evening the entire club attended a moving picture show and thus disposed of several hours that might otherwise have proved difficult to get through. A motor-boat, no matter how large or luxurious, is not the most interesting place to live on in wet weather.

The next morning the mist had ceased, but the sun was hidden behind dark clouds and the world was still rather dreary. But plenty of hot coffee, some of Ossie's baking powder biscuits and the almost invariable fried bacon cheered them remarkably, and at a little past eight the order was given to weigh anchor and the two cruisers, the *Adventurer* showing the way, set forth across Buzzard's Bay for Edgartown.

It was a sixteen-mile run to the channel between Nonamesset Island and the mainland, and Steve followed the steamboat course closely. The chart showed many rocks and ledges in the first six miles, but neither of the cruisers drew enough to make it necessary for their skippers to worry. There was rough water, however, and Joe was seen to look anxiously toward the after cabin. A flukey breeze came out of the southeast and made sweaters comfortable. The shore of Naushon Island was grey and indistinct when the *Adventurer* straightened out for the run across the bay. Behind her the *Follow Me* plunged gallantly, doing her fourteen miles without a murmur. As they neared Penzance the sea moderated and they swung into the channel on an almost even keel. Good harbours beckoned, and the plan of lying by until after dinner was discussed and finally abandoned. Edgartown was only another hour's sail and it would be better to keep on and lie in there for dinner. But when the *Adventurer* had passed into Vineyard Sound Steve began to wish he had waited. A bank of grey mist hid the island toward which they were headed and he feared they would find themselves in it before they could reach the nearest harbour, which was Vineyard Haven. But since the *Adventurer* had already left Wood's Holl two miles behind and Vineyard Haven Harbour was only some four miles further it seemed silly to turn back. There was always the chance that the fog would blow off, besides. Nevertheless Steve frowned dubiously through the moist pane ahead and, without saying anything of his fears to the rest, drew the throttle a few notches down and kept the *Adventurer* close to her course. Behind, the *Follow Me* speeded up as well and the two boats hurried for where, out of sight in the grey void ahead, West Chop pointed a blunt nose to sea.

But it was a losing race, for ten minutes later Steve saw that the fog bank was rolling down upon them and from somewhere to the eastward came the dismal hoot of a steamer feeling her way along. Joe, too, saw what they were in for and turned anxiously to Steve. "That's fog, isn't it?" he asked.

Steve nodded. "Get the fog-horn ready, will you? We don't want anyone bumping into us. I'm going to slow down to six miles. There's too much water here to drop anchor in." He eyed the advancing fog distastefully and then shrugged his shoulders. "You've got to learn some time, I suppose, Joe, and here's where I learn to make harbour by the compass. Now we're in it!"

At that instant the grey mist enveloped them silently, chillingly. Joe drew a long wail from the fog-horn and in response a similar but higher-keyed wail came through the fog from the *Follow Me*. And at the same moment the other members of the ship's company stuck inquiring heads through the companion ways.

"Hello," exclaimed Perry. "Fog! Gee, that's exciting! Say, you can't see a thing, can you? Look, fellows, the boat hasn't any bow!"

"Nor any stern," added Han. "You can almost taste the stuff. Say, Steve, isn't it hard to steer in a fog?"
"Not a bit," answered Steve cheerfully. "Steering's perfectly easy. The only trouble is to steer right."

"To-o-ot!" said the fog-horn and was answered from astern.

Then somewhere to the south-eastward a siren sent a wailing cry, subdued by distance. The fog settled on everything and shone on the boys' sweaters in little beads of moisture. The *Adventurer* seemed to be standing still, for, with nothing to judge by, progress was made known only by the slow lazy throb of the engine. Even the water alongside was scarcely discernible. Joe pulled the lever of the fog-horn again, and this time, beside the response from the *Follow Me*, an answering bellow came across the water.

"A steamer," muttered Steve, peering uselessly into the grey void. "She's a good ways off, though. Give her another pull, Joe."

Again the *Adventurer* proclaimed her position but there was no answer from the steamer. "She doesn't seem very talkative," said Phil. "How fast are we going, Steve?"

"Six."

"And how far is Edgartown?"

"About twelve, but we're not going there. I'm trying to make Vineyard Haven. It's only about two miles." He glanced puzzledly at the compass and moved the wheel a fraction. "There's a jetty comes out there and I guess we'd better give it a good wide berth." Collars were pulled up to keep the moisture from creeping down necks, and Perry begged to be allowed to manipulate the fog-horn. He went at it whole-souledly and Steve had to curb his enthusiasm. "Once a minute will do, Perry," he said. "You sound like a locomotive scaring a cow off the track."

"How do you know there isn't a cow ahead?" demanded Perry. "Or a whale? Gee, wouldn't it be a surprise if we bust right into a whale? Who would get the worst of it, Steve?"

"I guess we would. Shut up a minute, fellows, please!"

Silence held the bridge deck, silence save for the subdued purr of the engine under their feet and the drip, drip of the drops from the awning edge. Steve peered anxiously ahead, his senses alert. At last:

"Hear anything?" he asked.

They all said no.

"I guess I was mistaken then," Steve explained, "but I could have sworn I heard surf." He leaned over the chart. "This doesn't show anything, though, nearer than the land. Toot your horn, Perry."

Perry obeyed. At long intervals the unseen, distant steamer bellowed her warning and more frequently the *Follow Me* groaned dismally on a hand horn. It was ten minutes later, perhaps, when Steve suddenly swung around and looked back past the bow of the dingey on the after cabin roof.

"That's funny!" he exclaimed. "The *Follow Me* sounded away over there!" He looked anxiously at the compass, hesitated and shook his head. "If I didn't know this thing was all right, fellows, I'd say it was crazy. Or if there was a strong current here -" His voice dwindled away to a murmur as he studied the chart again. Just then the *Follow Me's* fog-horn sounded and it was undeniably further away and well over to port. "Either he's off his course or I am," muttered Steve. "And I simply don't see how I can be. Give them a long one, Perry!"

Perry sent a frantic wail across the water and they listened intently. But no reply came from the *Follow Me*. Instead, from somewhere off their port bow travelled the steamer's bellow. That, too, seemed considerably further away. Then the distant siren sounded, and after that there was silence again. But the silence lasted only a moment, for before anyone could hazard a conjecture as to the *Follow Me's* erratic behaviour, Phil's voice arose warningly.

"Listen, Steve!" he cried. "Isn't that surf I hear?"

CHAPTER VII

STEVE TAKES HER IN

Steve's hand flew to the clutch as the rest joined Phil at the side of the boat, and, in the grey silence that ensued, strained their ears.

"You're right," said Neil, after an instant. "There's surf there, or I'm a Dutchman. And it isn't far away."

Steve, who had handed the wheel to Joe, nodded. "It's surf, all right," he agreed, "but it hasn't any business there. What are you going to do when you can't depend on the chart? Well, the only thing for us to try is another direction." He swung the wheel well to port and slid the clutch in gently and, with the engine throttled down, the *Adventurer* nosed forward once more. "Phil, beat it out to the bow and keep your ears open, will you? Watch that deck, though; it's slippery." An anxious silence held for several minutes. Then Phil's voice came from the fog-hidden bow:

"Surf dead ahead, Steve!" he called.

"Can you see anything?" shouted Steve as he again disengaged.

"No, but I can hear the waves breaking."

They all could now that the propeller had stopped churning. Steve gazed dazedly from fog to compass and from compass to chart, and finally shook his head helplessly.

"It's too much for me, fellows," he said. "I'm going back as straight as I know how, or -" He stopped. "Hang it, there can't be land on *all* sides!" He pulled the bow still further to port and again started. "Keep your ears open, Phil," he called. "I'll run her as slow as she'll go. If you hear the surf plainer, shout."

The *Adventurer* went on again. After a moment Han, leaning outboard over the deck rail, said: "It's not so loud, Steve. I think we're going away from it slowly."

"Or else running parallel," suggested Perry. "Anyhow, it isn't any nearer."

Another minute or two passed, with all hands listening intently. Then Phil sounded another warning. "Hold up, Steve! I may be crazy, but I'll swear there's surf dead ahead again!"

Steve motioned to Joe and, yielding the wheel after throwing out the clutch again, swung around a stanchion and crept cautiously along the roof of the main cabin and galley until he reached Phil's side. Then, dropping to his knees and steadying himself by the flag-pole, he listened. Quite plainly and, as it seemed, from alarmingly nearby, came the gentle *swish-swash* of tiny waves breaking on a beach. In the fog it was difficult to tell whether the sound came from directly ahead or from starboard. At all events, when Steve turned his head to port the sound was certainly at his right or behind him.

"I'll try it again," he said. "You stay here, Phil." He climbed back to the bridge deck. "Perry, are you working that fog-horn?" he demanded. "If you aren't, get busy with it!" Once more the cruiser picked up and stole forward, her nose slowly swinging around to port. Steve had given up watching the compass now. All he wanted to do was find clear water. The *swish* of surf died away by degrees as the *Adventurer* edged cautiously along and, after five minutes, Steve gave a sigh of relief. "I guess we're all right now," he muttered to Joe, "but I'm going to keep her just moving. We might anchor, I suppose, but it's dollars to doughnuts we'd have to spend the night here; wherever here is," he added, scowling resentfully at the chart. "Look here, Joe." He reached forward and laid a finger on the map. "Here's where we were, or where we ought to have been, when we heard the surf first. According to this we were a good mile from the shore and the only shoal is that one and it's marked six feet at mean low water. There's a black-and-red spar buoy there, as you see, but we haven't sighted it. Now, what I want to know is how the dickens we could have got a mile off our course to starboard. Also, if we are off our course, where are we? Unless we've slipped over the beach and got into that pond down there -"

"Steve! Back up! We're running on the rocks!"

It was the frenzied voice of Phil in the bow. Steve thrust Joe aside and seizing the clutch put it quickly into neutral.

"Bring the boat-hook here!" shouted Phil. "Reverse, Steve! Hard!"

But Steve had already slammed the clutch into reverse and pulled down the throttle. A mighty thrashing and foaming sounded astern and the *Adventurer* trembled, hesitated and began to churn her way backward. Perry, boat-hook in hand, was sliding and stumbling along the wet deck. He reached the bow just in time to see the menacing face of a high stone jetty disappear again into the mist. Phil, clinging to the flag-pole, was sprawled on the deck with his legs stretched out to fend the boat off.

"Just in time!" he muttered, pulling himself back to safety. "Did you see it, Perry!"

"Did I see it? I almost fell overboard! That's enough, Steve!"

The *Adventurer* stopped going astern and Steve called anxiously from the wheel. "What was it, Phil?" he questioned.

"A breakwater about ten feet high! We almost hit it!"

"A breakwater!" Steve turned swiftly to the chart. "Then I know where we are at last! Look here, Joe!" He pointed. "We're cornered in here, see? Here's the shore on that side and the jetty dead ahead of us. How we got here I don't know, but here we are. If we can find the end of the jetty we're all right. Keep that horn going, Perry!"

"Why not drop an anchor where we are?" asked Joe.

"We could do that, of course, but here's the harbour right around the end of the jetty. Seems to me we might as well get in there, Joe."

"All right," agreed the other doubtfully, "but this feeling around in the dark is making me nervous. First thing we know we'll - um - we'll be running into the First National Bank or the Congregational Church or something! Still, if you think we can find our way, all right. I'm game."

Steve eyed the compass thoughtfully and in silence for a moment. Then: "You still there, Phil?" he called.

"Yes."

"Keep your eyes and ears open. I'm going to try to run along the side of the jetty and find the harbour. If you see a red spar buoy, sing out. Sing out if you see anything at all. Everyone keep a watch. We're going to eat dinner in the harbour or know why!"

The cruiser moved slowly on once more, her nose turning sharply. Then she paused, went back and again moved forward, Steve turning the wheel slowly with his eyes on the compass. "Now watch on the starboard side, Phil!" he called.

"Which is that? My right?"

"Yes, you land-lubber! Hear anything?"

"N-no! I didn't *hear* anything before until we were almost on the breakwater. Sometimes I think I can hear -"

Phil's voice died away to silence.

"Hear what?" asked Steve.

"Well, water sort of lapping. It may be against our boat, though."

"Neil, you go forward, too, will you?" said Steve. Neil joined Phil and for some minutes the *Adventurer* stole quietly along through the grey void with little sound save the slow working of the engine below deck and the lazy thud of the propeller. It was so quiet that when Perry suddenly worked the fog-horn Han almost fell over the wet rail on which he was sitting. It was Ossie who broke the silence finally.

"Well, I guess we've got to eat, whether we run ashore or stay afloat. I'm going to put some potatoes on."

"All right," replied Steve quietly. "But if you feel a bump, put out your alcohol flame the first thing you do, Ossie."

"Sure, but you can bet I won't wait down there to see whether the potatoes are done!"

"How about it, you chaps?" asked Steve presently.

"Don't hear a thing," answered Phil.

"All right. I'm going to bring her around now. Yell the minute you see anything. You needn't worry. She's only crawling and I'll have her going astern before you can shout twice."

Very slowly Steve moved the wheel to starboard. In the stillness they could hear the gear creak under the deck. No warning came from the two lookouts and, after a moment, Steve again turned gingerly. For all the watchers could tell, the *Adventurer* never altered her course, but Steve, his gaze on the compass card, knew that she was headed now straight east. Now and then he peered questioningly forward, but his gaze was defeated by the fog. At intervals Perry sent a groaning wail from the fog-horn. Presently Steve heard the boys talking on the bow and in a moment Neil's voice hailed him:

"Surf off to starboard, Steve! Not very near, though."

The others listened, but there was just enough noise from the engine to drown the sound heard by the lookouts.

"Tell me if it gets louder," called Steve. "Still hear it?"

"Not so well," answered Phil. "I think we're going away from it."

"Waves against the end of the jetty," explained Steve. "I think we're all right now." He moved the wheel over slowly, spoke by spoke. "Keep your horn going, Perry. We're entering the harbour. Watch for buoys, fellows. Take it on this side, Joe."

Followed a dubious five minutes during which the only sounds that reached them from outside the boat were distant fog signals and, once, the unmistakable moo of a cow!

"Gee," murmured Perry, "that's the best thing I've heard all day! That means we really are in the harbour, doesn't it?"

"Might be a sea-cow," suggested Ossie, from the companion.

"Ready with the bow anchor!" called Steve.

Han scuttled forward into the mist. "All right, sir!" he announced in his best nautical manner.

Steve disengaged the clutch. There was a moment of silence

aboard the *Adventurer*. Then: "Over with it, Han," directed Steve. There was a splash, followed by the rasping of the cable through the chock and then a cheerful whistle from the crew as he made fast. "About eighteen feet, Steve, I should say," he called.

"Sixteen," corrected the Captain gravely. Joe smiled.

"Mean it?" he asked.

Steve nodded and put a finger on the chart. "We're right here," he said. Then he covered the compass and drew down the lid of the chart box and stretched his arms luxuriously. "That's over with," he added, "and I'm glad of it! How about dinner, Ossie?"

"On the fire, Cap! Ready in five minutes."

"Then I'm going to get into a dry shirt. I'm soaked through. Some of you chaps pull the side curtains down on the port side. We might as well keep as dry as we can."

"Looks to me as if the fog was rolling in from the starboard, though," said Han.

"Yes, it's coming from the southeast, but we'll swing around in a few minutes because the tide's coming in. Wonder where the *Follow Me* is."

"Harry would probably make for harbour, too, wouldn't he?" asked Joe, following the other down to the cabin. "I wouldn't be surprised if we found them here when the fog clears."

A yacht, hidden somewhere in the fog ahead, sounded eight bells and was instantly echoed from further away. "Great Scott!" exclaimed Steve. "Is it twelve already?"

Joe nodded, glancing at the ship's clock at the end of the cabin. "Two minutes after if our clock's right. Say, Steve, the next time we go out in a fog we'll - um - we won't go, eh?"

"Not while I'm running this hooker," agreed Steve with intense conviction. "Now that it's over, Joe, I don't mind telling you that I was a bit worried. I wanted like anything to drop anchor back there by the jetty."

"Why didn't you then?"

"I don't quite know," replied the other thoughtfully, "but I think it was chiefly because I didn't like to be beaten."

"Dinner!" called Ossie from the forward cabin. "All hands to dinner! Get a move on!"

CHAPTER VIII

PERRY LOSES HIS WAY

They stayed aboard all that day, for the fog held tight, and, if Steve's calculations were right, the *Adventurer* lay well down toward the entrance to the harbour and the nearest settlement was a good mile and three-quarters away. None of the seven felt sufficiently ambitious to put out for shore in that smother of mist. They managed to pass the time without much trouble, however. There was always the graphophone, although they were destined to become rather tired of the records, and Steve, Joe, Han and Neil played whist most of the afternoon. Phil curled up on a couch and read, and Ossie and Perry, after having a violent argument over the proper way to make an omelet decided to settle the question then and there. By the time the two omelets were prepared the whist players were ready to stop and the entire ship's company partook of the rival concoctions and decided the matter in favour of Ossie.

"Although," explained Joe, "I'm not saying that Perry's omelet is bad. If he had remembered to put a little salt in it -"

"I did!" declared Perry resentfully. "You don't know a decent omelet when you see it. Look how light mine was! Why, it was twice as high as Ossie's!"

"That's just it," said Steve gravely. "It was so light that it sort of faded away before you could taste it. An omelet, Perry, should be substantial and filling."

"That shows how much you know about it," jeered Perry.

"There were just as many eggs in mine as there were in his. Only I made mine with water and beat the eggs separately -"

"Ah, there it is, you see," drawled Joe. "You beat the poor little eggs. I'm surprised at you, Perry. Any fellow who will beat an inoffensive egg -"

"Huh, I found one that wasn't inoffensive by a long shot! Someone will have to get some eggs tomorrow, for there are only eight left."

"What!" Han viewed Perry in disgust. "Mean to say you went and used them all up making those silly omelets?"

"I notice you ate the silly omelets," said Ossie. "One egg apiece is enough for breakfast, isn't it?"

"Not for me. The doctor ordered two every morning. If I don't have two eggs for breakfast I shall mutiny."

"If you do you'll be put in irons," said Joe. "Or swung from the yard-arm. Say, how long before we're going to have something to eat, Ossie? I'm hungry. That egg thing sort of whetted my appetite."

"Gosh, you fellows would keep me cooking all the time," grumbled the steward. "It's only five, and we don't have supper until six. So you can plaguey well starve for an hour."

"Then I shall go to sleep and - um - forget the pangs of hunger. Move your big feet out of the way, Phil."

"I like your cheek, you duffer! Go on back to your own bunk."

"Too faint for want of food," murmured Joe, stretching himself out in spite of Phil's protests. "Someone sing to me, please."

Supper went very well, in spite of the mid-afternoon luncheon, and after that the riding light was set for the night, the hatches drawn shut and all hands settled down to pass the evening in whatever way seemed best. But bedtime came early tonight and, by half-past nine, with the sound of a distant siren coming to them at intervals and the yacht's bells chiming the hours and half-hours, all lights were out below and the *Adventurer* was wrapped in fog and silence.

The fog still held in the morning, although at times it took on a yellowish tinge and made them hopeful that it would burn off. Steve said it was not quite so thick, but no one else was able to see much difference in it. Han managed to subsist on one egg, in spite of gloomy predictions, but after breakfast he and Perry decided to paddle ashore and find a place where they could purchase more. They tried to add to the party, but no one else wanted to go, and so they disappeared into the mist about nine o'clock, agreeing to be back at ten-thirty, at which time, unless the fog should have lifted, those aboard the boat were to sound the whistle.

They landed on a narrow beach after a short row, and, stumbling through a fringe of coarse sand, discovered a lane leading inland. They stopped and strove to remember the location of the boat, and then followed the lane. The fog was amber-hued now and the morning was fast losing its chill. Perry broke into song and Han into a tuneless whistle that seemed to give him a deal of satisfaction. They soon found a main-travelled road and, after fixing the turn-off in their minds, wheeled to the left.

"It would be a fine joke if we couldn't find the dingey again," chuckled Han.

"I think you've got a punk idea of humour," responded Perry. "Anyway, all we'd have to do is find the beach and keep along until we barked our skins on the boat. Bet you, though, this pesky fog will be gone in an hour."

The road left the shore presently and the travellers found that the fog was thinner and sometimes lifted entirely over small spaces, and it wasn't long before they stopped to take off their jackets and swing them across their arms. Possibly they passed houses, but they saw none, and the only incident occurred when the sound of wheels came to them from the highway ahead and, presently, a queer, old-fashioned two-wheeled chaise drawn by a piebald, drooping-eared horse passed slowly from the mist ahead to the mist behind. The boys gazed at it in wonderment, too interested in the equipage itself to heed the occupants. When it was out of sight again Han ejaculated: "Well, I'll be switched, Perry! I didn't suppose there was one of those things left in the world!"

"Neither did I. And there won't be pretty quick, I guess, for it looked and sounded as if it would fall to pieces before it got to - to wherever it's going. Bet you anything that was the deacon's one-horse chaise in the poem!"

> "*Have you heard of the wonderful one-hoss shay*
> *That was built in such a logical way*
> *It ran a hundred years to a day?*"

quoted Han. "Wouldn't that look funny alongside a Rolls-Royce, Perry?"

"It would look funny alongside a flivver," answered the other. "Say, how far do we have to walk? Seems to me we've done about five miles already."

"Rot! We haven't walked more than a mile. Not being able to see things makes it seem farther, I guess." The encouraging sound of a cow mooing reached them the next minute. "That must be the one we heard yesterday," said Han. "I suppose there's just one on the island and it's set to go off at the same time every day."

"If there's a cow over there," said Perry, staring into the fog, "maybe there's a farmhouse. Let's have a look."

"All right, but we're just as likely to walk into a swamp as find a house."

But a very few steps off the highway put them on a narrow lane and presently the big bulk of a barn loomed ahead. The house was soon located and ten minutes later, having purchased two quarts of milk and four dozen eggs, they retraced their steps. The fog had now apparently changed its mind about lifting, for the yellow tinge had gone and the world was once more grey and chill. They donned their coats again and, carrying their precious burdens, trudged on. Occasionally a puff of air came off the sound and the fog blew in trailing wreaths before them. When they had walked what they considered to be the proper distance they began to watch for that lane. And after they had watched for it for a full quarter of an hour and had walked a deal farther than they should have they reached the entirely justifiable conclusion that they were lost!

Perry set down the battered milk can on which they had paid a deposit of twenty-five cents, took a long breath and, viewing the encompassing fog, exclaimed melodramatically: "Lost on Martha's Vineyard, or The Mystery of the Four Dozen Eggs!"

"Well, we won't starve for awhile," laughed Han. "Say, where *is* that lane we came up, anyway? Think we've passed it?"

"About ten miles back," sighed Perry. "Come on and let's try dead reckoning. The beach is over there somewhere and if we can find it -"

"Great! But when we have found it, which way shall we go?"

Perry pushed his hat back and thoughtfully scratched his head. "Give it up!" he said at last. "You might go one way and I another. Anyway, let's find the old beach."

They scrambled across a wall into a bush-grown tract, Han discovering in the process that he had chosen a place prettily bedecked with poison-ivy. "That does for me," said Han gloomily. "I'll have a fine time of it now for a couple of weeks. I can't even look at that stuff without getting poisoned!"

"Maybe it didn't see you," said Perry cheerfully. "In this fog -"

"Don't be a silly goat," interrupted the other fretfully. "I tell you I'll be all broken out tomorrow! And it's perfectly beastly, too. You have blisters all over you and they itch so you can hardly stand it."

"Too bad," said Perry, trying to sound sympathetic but failing because he caught his foot in a bramble at the moment and almost pitched on his face.

"Well," continued Han, more cheerfully, "there's one good thing. Salt water is fine to bathe in when you have ivy poisoning, and there'll be plenty of that around."

"Sure; and it won't cost you a cent, either." They reached the beach then and gazed hopelessly about them as they crossed the softer sand. "If only they'd blow their old whistle we'd know where we are."

"If I had some alcohol I might backen it," observed Han.

"Alcohol? Backen what?"

"The ivy poison."

"Oh! Well, there's plenty of alcohol on board. Wonder what time it is," Perry drew out his watch and whistled surprisedly. "Only a quarter to ten, Han! We couldn't have walked very far, after all. And they won't signal us until ten-thirty. Here, I'm going this way."

"It's the alkali that counteracts the poison," explained Han. "They say that if you can bathe the places in alcohol soon after you come in - in contact with the ivy -"

"For the love of Pete!" exclaimed Perry. "Forget about it, Han! You'll worry yourself to death over that poison-ivy. Maybe it didn't bite you, after all."

"Of course it did!" replied the other resentfully. "It always does. If I had some alcohol, though -"

"Well, come on and get some. We've got to find the boat first, haven't we?"

"Yes, but I don't think it's that way."

"Then you try the other way, and if you find it, sing out so I'll hear you."

"All right." They separated, each following the edge of the water, and presently Perry's voice rang out. "Here she is, Han!" he called. A faint hail answered him and Perry stowed the milk-can in the bow of the little boat and seated himself to wait. A few minutes later, as Han still tarried, he shouted again. This time there was no reply however, and Perry muttered impatiently and found a more comfortable position. When some five minutes more had passed he got to his feet and yelled at the top of his lungs. "Get a move on, Han! The milk's getting sour and I'm getting cold!" he shouted. An answering cry came from closer by, but what it was that Han said Perry couldn't make out. He turned his coat collar up, plunged hands in pockets and viewed the grey mist scowlingly. Then he began to listen for footsteps crunching the sand. But no sound save the lapping of water on the beach and the creaking of a boom on an unseen boat reached him.

"It would serve him right to leave him here," he muttered resentfully. "Anyway, I'm not going to yell at him any more. I suppose he's so taken up with his poison-ivy business that he can't think of anything else. Wonder if I got into that stuff, too!" The idea was distinctly unwelcome. He thought he recalled brushing through leaves as he crossed the wall. He had never had any experience with poison-ivy and didn't know whether or not he was susceptible, but it seemed to him that there was a distinct itching sensation on his back. He squirmed uncomfortably. Then a prickly feeling on his left wrist set him to rubbing it. He examined the skin and, sure enough, it was quite red! He had it, too! You had blisters all over you, Han had said. Perry looked for blisters but found none. Still, he reflected miserably, it was probably too early for them yet. He suddenly found himself rubbing his right wrist too. And that, also, was distinctly inflamed looking, although not so red as the other. Gee, he'd ought to do something! Alcohol! That was it! He ought to bathe the places in alcohol! He jumped out of the dingey, pushed it down the beach into the water and sprawled across the bow. Then he shoved further off with an oar and sudsided onto a seat.

"Back in ten minutes for you, Han!" he shouted. "You wait here! I'll bring some alcohol!"

When a dozen choppy strokes had taken him out of sight of the shore his panic subsided a little and two thoughts came to him. The first was that he was treating Han rather scurvilly and the second was that he hadn't more than the haziest notion where the *Adventurer* lay! But, having embarked, he kept on. Probably ten or fifteen minutes wouldn't make much difference in Han's case, while, as for finding the cruiser, he would shout after he had rowed a little further and doubtless someone aboard would hear him.

So he went on into the mist, occasionally stopping to scratch a wrist or wiggle about on the seat in the endeavour to abate the prickling sensation in back or shoulders. It seemed to him now that he was infected from head to toes. Presently, having rowed some distance , he began to hail. " *Adventurer* ahoy! " he shouted, "O Steve! O Joe!"

He stopped rowing, rubbed a wrist, peered into the fog and waited. But no answering hail reached him. He lifted his voice again. "Ahoy! *Adventurer* ahoy! Are you all dead? Where are you?"

This time there was an answer, faint but unmistakable, and, somewhat to Perry's surprise, it came from almost behind him. "Shout again!" he called. "Where are you?"

"He-e-ere! Hurry up!" At least, that was what the answer sounded like. Perry grumblingly turned the boat around and rowed in the direction of the voice. "I suppose," he thought, "I rowed in a circle. I always did row harder with my right. But I don't see what they want me to hurry for. And they might blow their whistle if they had any sense."

"Shout again!" he yelled presently.

"Hello-o-o!" came a hail from somewhere back of the boat, and: "Come ahead!" called a voice from the fog in front. Perry exploded.

"Shut up, one of you!" he called exasperatedly. "I can't row two ways at once! Where's the boat?" But his remarks evidently didn't carry, for all he got was another hail from behind. "All right," he muttered. "Why didn't you say so before?" He swung the dingey around a second time and rowed on a new course. "Wonder who the other chap was," he thought. "I dare say, though, there are boats all around here if a fellow could see them." A minute later he called again: "Come on, you idiots! Where are you?"

"Don't bust yourself," said a voice from almost over his shoulder. "And watch where you're going if you don't want to stave that boat in."

CHAPTER IX

SOUR MILK

Perry was so surprised that he almost fell off the seat, while, forgetting to obey injunctions, he let the dingey run until there was a sudden bump that toppled the milk-can over and nearly treated him the same way. He looked startledly about. Six feet away lay a black boat and a boy with a boat-hook was threatening him from the deck.

"You silly idiot!" called the boy impatiently. "Look where you're going! If I hadn't got you with the hook you'd have knocked half our paint off!"

The boy and the boat slowly vanished in the mist like a "fade-out" at the movies, before Perry found his voice. Then: "Who the dickens are you?" he gasped.

"I'm the man who put the salt in the ocean," replied the voice jeeringly. "Come on easy and I'll get you."

"Well, but - but - what boat's that?"

"U.S. Battleship *Pennsylvania*, Pride of the Navy! Come on, you lubber!"

Perry came on and again the boy with the boat-hook took form in the fog. "You're Cas Temple," said Perry stupidly. "That's the *Follow Me*!"

"Surest thing you know, son! Hello! Why, it's Perry Bush. I

thought you were Bert. What did you do with the fellows?"

"What fellows?" asked Perry, puzzled, as Cas pulled the dingey alongside the cruiser.

"Why, Bert and Wink and the rest of them."

"Haven't seen 'em."

"Haven't? Where'd you get the boat, then?"

"What boat?"

"That one! The one you're in! Say, are you dippy?"

"This is our boat and I got it -"

"Your boat nothing! That's our boat, you silly chump! Think I don't know our own tender?"

"Wh-what!" gasped Perry. "So it is! Then, where's mine! I mean ours? How did I get this one?"

"Search me! If you don't know, I'm blessed if I do," chuckled Caspar Temple. "You must remember something that's happened since yesterday morning!"

"Han and I went ashore," said Perry, staring puzzledly at the milk-can from which a tiny stream was trickling past the loosened stopper. "Then we went to look for our boat and I found this and I yelled to him and he didn't come and so I started back to the boat to get some -" Perry suddenly remembered his affliction. "Say, got any alcohol?" he asked anxiously.

"Alcohol? I don't know. Why?"

"I want some." Perry started to scramble out of the tender. "I got poisoned."

"Snake?" asked Cas hopefully and eagerly.

"Poison-ivy."

"Oh!" The other's voice held keen disappointment. "Well, what do you want alcohol for?"

"It's good for it," explained Perry, reaching the cockpit. "See if you've got any, will you, Cas?"

"Y-yes but, honestly, Perry, I wouldn't try it if I were you."

"Why not!"

"Why - why, if you go and drink a lot of alcohol - Besides, I'm all alone here, and if you got - got troublesome -"

"Drink it, you silly goat! Who's going to drink it? I'm going to rub it on the places!"

"Oh, I see! That's different. I'll have a look, Perry." Cas was visibly relieved as he scrambled down to the cabin. Perry dropped into the dingey again and set the milk-can upright, and then, after another minute, Cas returned empty-handed. "I'm sorry," he said, "but we haven't a bit. Would peroxide do?"

"I don't know," answered Perry doubtfully. "Maybe. Hand it here and I'll give it a chance. Say," he continued as he laved his wrists, "did your crowd leave this boat on the beach?"

"I suppose so. That's where you found it, wasn't it! You'd better hustle back with it, too, for they said they'd be back about eleven. They went to Vineyard Haven."

"It's all well enough to say hustle back with it," replied Perry morosely, "but where's your pesky beach?"

"Why, over there," said Cas, pointing. "The way you came."

RALPH HENRY BARBOUR

"I came forty-eleven different directions," answered Perry. "All right, though. I'll try it. But I'm likely to be paddling around all day and night. Got anything to eat on board?" Cas found some cookies and these, with a glass of water, raised Perry's spirits. "Farewell," he said feelingly, as he shoved off again. "I die for my country."

"Did you fellows have any trouble finding this place yesterday?" asked Cas as the departing guest dropped the oars in the locks.

"Trouble?" Perry looked blank. "What sort of trouble?"

"Why, the fog, you know. We had an awful time finding the harbour."

"Oh, that!" Perry shrugged. "Why, we went straight for the jetty and didn't have any trouble at all finding it. But then we've got a navigator on our boat. So long!"

Perry discovered that rowing was raising a blister on each palm and that his arms were getting decidedly tired. The trouble with a dingey, he decided, was that while it might do excellently as a bathtub, it was certainly never meant for rowing. The oars were so short that the best strokes he was capable of sent the boat ahead scarcely more than three or four feet, and, being almost as broad as it was long, the tender constantly showed a tendency to go any way but straight ahead. While he had been aboard the *Follow Me* the fog had again taken on its amber hue and now was unmistakably thinning out. But it was still thick enough to hide objects thirty feet away and Perry couldn't for the life of him be certain that he was sending his craft toward the beach. To be sure he had started out in the general direction of the shore, as indicated by Cas, but there was always the possibility that he was rowing stronger with one oar than the other. He strove to curb that tendency and fancied he was succeeding, but when, after being afloat a good quarter of an hour, he still failed to see land or hear the break of waves on the beach he was both puzzled and annoyed. The sun pierced the mist hotly and he was soon panting and perspiring. He heartily wished that he had never agreed to accompany Han on the search for eggs. Presently he rested on his oars, and as he did so he heard voices quite close. He called.

"Hello, there! Where's the beach?"

"Here," was the answer.

He rowed on and in another minute land came abruptly out of the fog. Two blurred forms resolved themselves into men as Perry beached the dingey and tiredly dropped the oars. The men came toward him and proved, on nearer acquaintance, to be middle-aged and apparently natives. "Quite a fog," drawled one of them. "What boat you from, sir?"

"The *Adventurer*." Perry viewed the immediate foreground with misgiving. The beach looked more abrupt than he recalled it. "What beach is this?" he inquired.

"Well, I don't know as it's got any name exactly. What beach was you lookin' for?"

"The beach between Vineyard Haven and - and some other place."

"Oh, West Chop? Why, that's across the harbour, son. This is Eastville, this side."

Perry groaned. He had rowed in a half-circle then. Unless Cas had directed him wrong. Presently the true explanation came to him. The tide had turned between the time the *Follow Me's* crowd had gone ashore and the time that Perry had reached that boat, and Cas had not allowed for the fact that the cruiser had swung around! "Well," he said wearily, "I guess I've got to row across again."

"Too bad," sympathised one of the men. "It's most a mile. Guess, though, you'll be able to see your way pretty soon. This fog's burning off fast."

Out of sight of the men Perry again laid his oars down and reached behind him for the can of milk. It was rather warm, but it tasted good for all of that. Then, putting the wooden stopper back in place, he once more took up his task. Perhaps he might have been rowing around that harbour yet had not the fog suddenly disappeared as if by magic. Wisps of it remained here and there, but even as he watched them, they curled up and were burned into nothingness like feathers in a fire. He found himself near the head of a two-mile-long harbour. The calm blue water was rippling under the brushing of a light southerly breeze and here and there lay boats anchored or moored. While the fog had hidden the harbour he had supposed that not more than half a dozen craft were within sight, but now, between mouth and causeway, fully two dozen sailboats and launches dotted the surface. Over his shoulder was a little hamlet that was doubtless Vineyard Haven. Facing him was a larger community, and he decided that that would be Oak Bluffs. Half a mile down the harbour lay the *Adventurer* and, nearer at hand, the *Follow Me*. But what was of more present interest to Perry was a group of figures on the opposite beach. They appeared to be seated and there was that in their attitude which, even at this distance, told of dejection. So, reflected Perry, might have looked a group of marooned sailors. He sighed and bent again to his inadequate oars. He was under no misapprehension as to the sort of welcome awaiting him, but, like an early Christian martyr on the way to the arena, he proceeded with high courage if scant enthusiasm.

With the sun pouring down upon him, with his hands blistered, with his breath just about exhausted and his arms aching, he at last drew to the shore amidst a dense and unflattering silence. Five irate youths stepped into the tender and crowded the seats. Harry Corwin took his place beside Perry and relieved him of the port oar. Perry would have yielded the other very gladly, but none offered to accept it and he hadn't the courage to make the suggestion. The dingey floated off the sand again, headed for the *Follow Me,* and then the storm broke. It didn't descend all at once, however. At first there were muffled growls of thunder from Harry Corwin. Then came claps from Wink Wheeler. After that the elements raged about Perry's defenceless head, even "Brownie" supplying some fine lightning effects!

Perry gathered in the course of the uncomplimentary remarks directed toward him that the crowd, being unable to find the dingey where they believed they had left it, had spent some twenty minutes searching up and down the beach, that subsequently they had waited there in the fog for a good forty minutes more and that eventually Perry Bush would sooner or later come to some perfectly deplorable end and that for their part they didn't care how soon it might be. By the time the *Follow Me* was reached Perry was too worn out to offer any excuse. Cas, however, did it for him, and, as the others' tempers had somewhat sobered by then amusement succeeded anger. Perry faintly and vaguely described his wanderings about the harbour and the amusement increased. As dinner was announced about that time he was dragged to the cabin and propped in a corner of a bunk and fed out of hand. An hour later he was transported, somewhat recovered, to the *Adventurer* by Harry and Tom Corwin and Wink Wheeler and delivered, together with his precious can of milk, into the hands of his ship-mates.

The *Adventurer's* tender bobbed about at the stern and the first person Perry set eyes on as he scrambled onto the bridge deck was Han. Perry fixed him with a scathing gaze. "Where," he demanded, "did you get to, idiot?"

"Oh, I'll tell you about that," answered Han. "You see I was afraid about that poison-ivy and so I took a dip in the ocean. And -"

"But I called you and called!"

"Yes, and I answered a couple of times. And then I may have

had my head under water."

"A monstrous pity you didn't keep it there!"

"When," continued Han, "I went to look for you I couldn't find you. So I - so I came back here."

"Yes, you thought maybe I'd swum across, eh! Or found a boat?"

"Sure! You did find a boat, didn't you?"

"You make me tired," growled Perry amidst the laughter of the others. "And I hope that poison-ivy gets you good and hard!"

"I don't believe it took," replied Han gently, "Maybe it wasn't poison-ivy, after all!"

At that instant the outraged countenance of Ossie appeared in the companion way. "What," he demanded irately of Perry, "do you mean by bringing back half a gallon of sour milk?"

Perry looked despairingly about at the unsympathetic and amused faces and wandered limply aft to the seclusion of the cockpit.

The next morning the Adventure Club chugged around to Edgartown, and then, after putting in gasoline and water, set out at a little after eleven, on a fifty-mile run to Pleasant Bay.

CHAPTER X

THE *FOLLOW ME* DISAPPEARS

There had been talk of going through the Cape Cod Canal and so obviating the outside journey, but most of the voyagers thought that would be too tame and unexciting. Besides, a barge had managed to sink herself across the channel near the Buzzard's Bay end a week or so before and no one seemed to know for certain whether she had yet pulled herself out and gone on about her business, and, as Steve pointed out, they'd feel a bit foolish if they got to the canal entrance and had to turn back again. They had fair weather and light breezes all the way to New Harbour and from there, the next day, around the tip of the Cape to Provincetown. They dropped anchor off the yacht club landing at Provincetown at four o'clock Friday afternoon and went ashore as soon as the boats were berthed and sought the post-office. Provincetown had been selected as the first certain port of call and most of the thirteen boys found mail awaiting them. Only Neil, however, received tidings of importance, and his letter from his parents brought an exclamation of dismay to his lips.

"Anything wrong?" asked Ossie, sitting beside him on the rail of the hotel porch.

"Rotten," replied Neil disgustedly. "I've got to go home!"

"Go home!" echoed the other. "What for?"

"Dad's got to go to England on some silly business or other," explained Neil gloomily, "and he wants me to stay with

RALPH HENRY BARBOUR

mother. Of course I ought to. Mother's sort of an invalid and there's no one else. But it's rotten luck." He stowed the letter in his pocket and stared disappointedly at the passing traffic. "I was having a bully time, too," he muttered disconsolately.

"That's a shame," said Ossie sympathetically. "When will you have to go?"

"He wants me to meet him in New York Sunday. He sails early Monday morning. I suppose I'll have to go tomorrow. Guess I'd better get a time table and see how the trains run."

"Gee, I'm sorry," murmured Ossie.

And so, for that matter, was every other member of the *Adventurer's* company for Neil was well liked. And the *Follow He's* crew were scarcely less regretful. A study of the railroad schedule showed that the next train for Boston left at five-fifty-five in the morning and that the only other train was at two-forty in the afternoon.

"Five-fifty-five's a perfectly punk time for a train to leave anywhere, even Provincetown," objected Neil. "And the two-forty will get me to Boston too late for anything but a midnight train to New York."

"Bother trains," said Steve. "We'll run you to Boston tomorrow in the boat. We can do it in four hours or so. If the *Follow Me* crowd want to stay here another day we'll wait for them at Boston, or we'll go on and meet them further up the shore."

"But I don't want to hurry you chaps away from the Cape," expostulated Neil. "You were going to Plymouth, weren't you?"

"Yes, we were, but there's nothing important about that. Hold on, though! I say, look up the Plymouth trains, Neil. There must be more of them from there and we can put you across to

Plymouth in a couple of hours."

They found that a train leaving Plymouth at ten would put Neil in Boston shortly after eleven, in plenty of time for the one o'clock express to New York, and so it was decided that the *Adventurer* was to leave her present port at seven in the morning. The *Follow Me* was to follow more leisurely and the boats would spend the next night at Plymouth. Neil and Ossie went off to send telegrams and the others roamed around the town until it was time for supper. Afterwards Neil packed his belongings in two pasteboard laundry boxes, having no bag with him, and constantly bewailed his ill-fortune. Later the *Follow Me* crowd came over and they had quite a jolly evening and Neil cheered up vastly.

The next morning dawned clear and hot and, after an early breakfast, the *Adventurer* weighed anchor. The *Follow Me's* whistle signalled good-bye until they were half-way to Long Point and the *Adventurer* replied. Once around the point the boat headed across the wide bay for the mainland at a good sixteen-mile clip. The voyage was uneventful and Manomet Hill was soon sighted. Then Plymouth Beach stretched before them and presently they were rounding the head and pointing the *Adventurer's* nose for the town. There was still the better part of an hour left after the anchor was dropped and they all tumbled into the dingey and found a landing and spent the next three-quarters of an hour rambling around the historic town, Ossie and Perry bearing Neil's strange-looking luggage. Neil insisted on viewing Plymouth Rock, declaring that he might never get another opportunity, and after that there was not much time left to them. They installed Neil on the train impressively, stowed his luggage around him and then took up positions outside the window, where, to the mingled curiosity and amusement of other travellers, they conducted farewell exercises. These included an entirely impromptu and unsolicited duet by Perry and Han, a much interrupted speech by Joe, and, finally, as the train moved out of the station, a hearty Dexter cheer with three "Neils!" on the end. In such manner the *Adventurer* lost her cabin boy and the ranks of the club were depleted by one.

Neil's departure left a hole and as the others returned from the station they spoke of him rather as though he had passed on to a better world, recalling his good points and becoming quite sad in a cheerful way. In view of their bereavement, they decided to have luncheon at a hotel and during that meal recovered their spirits. More sight-seeing followed, but the day was a hot one and by half-past three they had had enough and so returned to the landing and pulled back to the cruiser. Steve, who had supplied himself with yesterday's New York and Boston papers, pre-empted a seat on the bridge deck and stretched himself out on it, his legs crooked over the railing. The others found places in the shade as best they could and talked and watched for the *Follow Me* and listened to occasional snatches of news from Steve. There was practically no breeze and the afternoon was uncomfortably hot even under the awning. Joe finally solved the difficulty of keeping cool by disappearing below and presently re-emerging in his swimming trunks and dropping overboard. That set the fashion, and they all went in save Steve, who was too absorbed in his papers to know whether he was warm or not. The *Follow Me* came up the harbour just before five and tooted a greeting as she swung around to a berth near the *Adventurer*. The fellows, who were still in bathing attire, swam across to her, and very shortly their ranks were increased by just half a dozen more. The sight of Steve's feet hanging over the canvas was too much for Perry and he yielded to temptation. Swimming up very quietly he deftly pulled off one of Steve's "sneakers" and, in defiance of the owner's protests, they played ball with it until the inevitable happened and it sank out of sight before Wink Wheeler could dive for it. "Brownie" said then that Steve might as well let them have the other one, since one shoe was no use to him, but Steve's reply was not only non-compliant but actually insulting in its terms. He took off the other "sneaker" and laid on it.

That bath left them feeling both refreshed and hungry and Ossie had a hard time finding enough for them to eat. Perry described the astonishment of some Plymouth fisherman when he opened a codfish some fine day and discovered a rubber-soled shoe inside. "You'll read all about it in the paper, Steve, and won't you laugh!" he added.

Steve, who had been forced to don a pair of leather shoes, didn't seem to anticipate any great amount of amusement, however, and suggested that it would be a gentlemanly act if Perry would hie himself to a store and purchase a pair of number 8 "sneakers," a suggestion which Perry weighed carefully and discarded. "You see," he explained, "it wouldn't be fair to make me spend my hard-earned money for two 'sneakers' when I only lost one. If the store would sell me half a pair, Steve, I'd make good in a minute, but you see my point of view, don't you?"

Steve didn't seem to.

While they were still at table Harry Corwin's voice was heard and Ossie investigated by the simple expedient of climbing on top of the galley locker and thrusting his head through the open hatch. "He wants to know if we'll go to the movies with them," said Ossie, ducking back into sight.

"Surest thing you know," agreed Perry.

"We might as well, eh?" asked Joe. "It'll be beastly hot, though."

"I'll go if they've got Charlie Chaplin," said Han. "Ossie, ask him if they have, please."

"He says he doesn't know," responded Ossie after an exchange of remarks. "I told them we'd go, though," he added, dropping to the floor. "They're going to wait for us on the landing in half an hour."

"Half an hour!" grumbled Perry. "You told them that so I couldn't get enough to eat, you stingy beggar! Got anything more out there?"

"Great Jumping Jehosaphat!" ejaculated Ossie wildly. "I've cooked two messes of potatoes and toasted a hundred slices of bread -"

"Oh, all right. Bring on the dessert, then."

"The dessert's on now," answered Ossie shortly. "Cookies and jelly. That's all you get, Piggie."

"Won't we have to buy some more grub pretty soon?" asked Steve.

Ossie nodded and glanced darkly at Perry. "If *he* stays around we will," he answered. "We've got enough for three or four days yet, though. Better have some canned stuff, I guess. And some flour and sugar."

"How's the treasury, Phil?" inquired Han.

"Still holding out. Where's the next stop, Steve?"

"We said Portsmouth, but Harry wants to put in at Salem. I don't suppose it matters much."

"Then we cut out Boston altogether?"

"Why, yes, it's out of the way a bit. Besides, we didn't start out on this cruise to visit cities."

"We started out to look for adventures," said Perry sadly, "but I don't see many of them coming our way."

"What do you call adventures?" asked Han. "Didn't you have a fine time being lost in the fog the other day?"

"Huh!" replied Perry, scraping the last of the jelly from the glass. "Being lost in the fog isn't an adventure. It's just plain punk. What I mean is - is pirates and - and desert islands and - and that sort of thing."

"You were born a hundred years or so too late," said Joe, shaking his head. "Toss me a cookie, Han. Thanks. If you saw a pirate, Perry, you'd - um - you'd drop dead."

"If I saw a pirate," replied Perry indignantly, "I'd - um - live as long as you would! Besides, I've got a perfect right to drop dead if I want to."

"Go ahead," said Joe lightly. "Any time you like, old chap."

"The reason I spoke of Boston," reverted Phil, "was that I thought it might be a good place to buy our supplies. There's no use paying any more for them than we have to and going broke before the cruise is half over."

"Yes, but don't forget that gasoline's pretty expensive stuff these days, Phil," said Steve. "I guess we'd burn up enough gas getting to Boston to make up for any saving on supplies, eh? I suppose there are stores in Salem."

"Thought it burned up awhile ago," said Han.

"Part of it did, but I don't suppose it stayed burned up, you idiot. What time is it? We'd better beat it for shore."

"Right-o," agreed Han. "I hope they have Charlie Chaplin, though."

By some strange inadvertency, however, Mr. Chaplin's eccentric person was missing from the screen. In spite of that, though, Han managed to enjoy the evening. Afterwards Perry suggested light refreshments and they set out in search of a lunch counter. But anyone who knows Plymouth will realise the hopelessness of their search. After roaming around the quiet and deserted streets and at last being assured by a policeman that their quest was worse than idle they went back to the tenders. "I suppose," said Perry disgustedly, "they close all the stores early so they can go to the movies. I wish now we'd had some soda at that drug store where the man had insomnia."

"We've got food on board," said Ossie. "I'll fix up some sandwiches. I wish you'd get enough to eat for once, though," he added as he took his place in the dingey. "Don't they ever feed you at home, Perry?"

"Huh, I'll bet you're as hungry as I am! What are they yelping about over there?"

The other tender had left the landing a moment before the *Adventurer's* boat and now its occupants were heard shouting confusedly across the moonlit water.

"Can you make out what they're saying?" asked Steve of the rest.

"Just nonsense, I guess," answered Phil, tugging at his oar.

"Stop rowing a minute and listen," Steve directed. "Now then!"

"Something about the boat," murmured Han. "I can't make it out, though."

"By Jove, I can!" exclaimed Steve. "The *Follow Me's* gone! She must have slipped her anchor or dragged or something. Row hard, fellows!"

CHAPTER XI

PURSUIT

Whatever had happened, one fact was plain, and that was that the smaller of the two cruisers was not swinging at anchor where they had left her. Nor could they see her anywhere. That she had dragged her anchor was impossible, since the harbour was almost land-locked and the night was still, with hardly enough breeze to stir the water. After the first few minutes of stunned surprise the twelve boys, gathered on the *Adventurer*, held council. It was Phil who eventually summed up the situation quietly and tersely as follows:

"The boat's gone. She isn't in the harbour, because if she were we could see her. Either she's been taken off as a joke or stolen. I can't imagine anyone doing it as a joke. In any case it's up to us to find her. We went ashore about eight, and it's now ten to eleven. It's probable that whoever swiped her waited until we were safely ashore and out of the way. I mean, they probably allowed us at least half an hour."

"They were probably watching us," suggested Steve.

"Why didn't they take this one instead of the other?" asked Cas Temple.

"Perhaps," replied Steve, "because they found the control locked. All they had to do on the *Follow Me* was break the padlock on the companion way doors. Still, that's just a guess. They may have preferred the *Follow Me* for some other reason."

RALPH HENRY BARBOUR

"Never mind that," said Joe impatiently. "The question now is how we're to find her. Go ahead, Phil."

"I was going to suggest that we inquire among the other boats between here and the harbour entrance. Two or three still have lights aboard. Maybe they saw the *Follow Me* pass out."

"Somebody look after the tenders," said Steve briskly. "Haul ours out and tie the other astern. Give her a short line, so she won't switch around and fill with water. All ready, Joe?"

Five minutes later the *Adventurer* slid through the still water toward the mouth of the harbour. On her way she stopped twice to shout inquiries, and the second time a sleepy mariner, leaning, in pajamas across the rail of a small launch, supplied the information they sought.

"Yes, there was a cruising motor-boat went by about nine, or a little after, headed toward the Pier Head. I didn't notice her much, but she was painted dark. Come to think of it, it must have been pretty nearly half-past, for I remember hearing three bells strike just afterwards."

"You didn't see her after she went by here?" asked Steve.

"No, I was getting ready for bed and saw her through a port. Anything wrong?"

"Nothing," replied Steve dryly, "except that she belongs to us and someone's evidently stolen her. Thanks very much. Good night."

"Good night," was the answer. "I hope you get her."

"Well, we know she got this far," said Joe, "but - um - which way did they take her when they got outside?"

"That's the question," said Harry Corwin. "They might have gone across to Provincetown and around the Cape, or taken her up the shore or down. I guess the best thing for us to do would be to hike back and give the alarm. If we telegraphed -"

"She went north," said Phil with conviction.

"How do you know?" demanded Joe.

"I don't *know*, but think a minute. If you were stealing a boat you'd want to keep out of sight with her, wouldn't you?"

"Suppose I should."

"Then you wouldn't mess around in Cape Cod Bay. You'd set a course as far from other craft and harbours as you could. If they went south they'd be among boats right along, and they'd know that we'd work the wires and that folks would be on the lookout."

"Then where," began Steve.

"Let's look at the chart from here north," said Phil. The cover of the chart box was thrust back and the lamp lighted and as many as could do so clustered about it. Phil traced a finger across Massachusetts Bay past the tip of Cape Ann. "There's clear sailing for ninety miles or so, straight to Portland, unless - How much gas has she aboard, Harry?"

"Only about twelve gallons." It was Tom Corwin who answered. "We were going to fill again in the morning."

"How far can she go on that?"

"Not more than seventy at ordinary speed, I guess. She's hard on gas."

"Good ! Then she'd have to put in at Gloucester or Newbury-port or somewhere."

"Unless she ducked into Boston Harbour," said Steve. "I dare say she could tuck herself away somewhere there quite safely. A coat of white paint would change her looks completely."

"That's possible," agreed Phil, "but painting a boat of that size would take a couple of days, wouldn't it? It doesn't seem to me that they'd want to take the chance."

"Then your idea is that they're on their way to Portland?"

"Somewhere up there. They'd argue that we wouldn't be likely to look for them so far away."

"Well, here we are," said Steve. "We've got to go one way or another." The rougher water outside was making the *Adventurer* dip and roll. "As far as I can see, Phil's theory is as good as another, or maybe better. Shall we try going north, fellows?"

No one answered until, after a moment's silence, Perry remarked philosophically: "I don't believe we'll ever see her again, but we can't stop here, and we were going northward anyhow."

Murmurs of agreement came from the others. The only dissentient voice was Bert Alley's. "*I* don't see your argument," he said. "If I had swiped the *Follow Me* I'd hike out for New York or some place like that and run her into some little old hole until I could either change her looks or sell her."

"And be nabbed on the way," said Joe.

"Not if I stayed at sea."

"But you couldn't stay at sea if you had only twelve gallons of gasoline aboard. Wherever she's going, she will have to put in for gas before long." Phil stared thoughtfully at the chart. "I'll allow," he went on, "that she may have gone any other direction but north. For that matter, she may be anchored just around the corner somewhere. It's all more or less guesswork.

But, looking at the probabilities, and they're all we've got to work on, I think north is the likeliest trail for us to take."

"Right-o," said Steve, turning the wheel and pointing the boat's slim bow toward Gurnet Point, "We've got to take a chance, fellows, and this looks like the best. In the morning we'll get busy with the telegraph and tell our troubles, but just now the best we can do is keep a sharp lookout and try to think we're on the right course. I'm going to speed her up, Joe, so you might dab some more oil and grease around your old engine."

"All right. You fellows will have to clear out of here, though, while I get this hatch up. Some of you might go forward and keep your eyes peeled. I don't suppose, however," he added as he pulled the engine hatch up, "that they'll show any lights on her."

"Not likely to," agreed Harry Corwin. "They'll run dark, probably, until they get near a harbour. Look for anything like a boat, fellows. It's a mighty good thing we've got this moonlight."

"Yes, and we'll have to make hay while the moon shines," added Wink Wheeler as he climbed out of Joe's way, "for it won't last much longer. It'll be as dark as pitch by one or two o'clock, I guess."

"Well, we've got a searchlight," said Perry.

"There's no need for more than three of us to stay up," said Steve. "I'll keep the wheel and Joe will stay here with me. Phil, you take the watch for a couple of hours and then wake someone else."

"Huh!" said Perry. "I'm not going to bed! Who wants to sleep, anyway?"

Apparently no one did, for although presently the dozen

fellows were distributed over the boat, not one went below. Phil and Han stretched themselves out at the bow, Steve, Joe, Harry and Tom Corwin and Cas Temple remained on the bridge deck and the rest of the company retired to the cockpit, from where, by looking along the after cabin roof, they had a satisfactory view of the course. Perhaps one or two of the boys did nod a little during the next two hours, but real slumber was far from the minds of any of them. The *Adventurer* was doing a good twenty miles an hour, the propeller lashing the water into a long foaming path that melted astern in the moonlight. Ossie busied himself in the galley about midnight and served hot coffee and bread-and-butter sandwiches. Only once was the *Adventurer* changed from her course, which Steve had laid for Gloucester, and then the light which had aroused their suspicions was soon seen to belong to a coasting schooner beating her way toward Boston. Of small boats there were none until, at about one o'clock, when the two white lights of Baker's Island lay west by north and the red flash on Eastern Point showed almost dead ahead, Phil called from the bow.

"Steve, there's something ahead that looks like a boat or a rock. Can you see it?"

"Which side?"

"A little to the left. Port, isn't it? Han doesn't see it, but -"

"I've got it," answered Steve. After a moment he added with conviction: "It's a boat. Has she changed her position, Phil?"

"Not while I've been watching. Looks as if she was going about the same way we are." The others came clustering forward from the stern to stare across the water at the dark spot ahead which, in the uncertain light of the setting moon, might be almost anything. If it was a boat, it showed no light. Anxiously the boys watched, and after a few minutes Steve announced with quiet triumph:

"We're pulling up on her, fellows, whoever she is!"

"She's the *Follow Me*," declared Harry Corwin. "She must be, or she wouldn't be running without lights."

"We'll know before long," said Steve. "I wish the moon would stay out a little longer, though. Joe, try the searchlight and see if you can pick her up."

But the craft ahead was a good mile away and the *Adventurer's* small searchlight was not powerful enough to bridge that distance with its white glare. "They're making for the harbour, anyway," said Harry Corwin, "and so she can't get away from us if we lose her now." Even as he ended the last pallid rays of the moon vanished and they found themselves in darkness save for the wan radiance of the stars. Lights unnoticed before sprang up in the gloom along the shore and a dim radiance in the sky showed where the town of Gloucester slumbered.

"If they double on us now we'll lose them," muttered Steve. "Put that light out, Joe. We can see better without it."

"How far off is the harbour?" asked Harry.

"About two miles. You can hear the whistle buoy. That white light to the left of the red flash is the beacon on the end of the breakwater." He moved the helm a trifle and examined the chart. "There are no rocks, anyway, and that's a comfort. I can't say I like this running at night. How far away was she when the moon went back on us, Harry?"

"Oh, three-quarters, at a rough guess."

"Nearer a mile and a quarter, I'd say. Well, if she doesn't dodge along shore we'll have her in the harbour. Always supposing, that is, that she really is the *Follow Me*."

"She can't be anything else," answered Harry. "No sensible skipper would go ploughing around at night without a light. Hello! Isn't that a light there now?"

"Where? Yes, you're right! She's lighted up at last! Afraid to go in without lights, I dare say, for fear of arousing suspicion. I'm getting to believe she *is* the *Follow Me*, Harry."

"I haven't doubted it once. Do you suppose she knows we're after her?"

"She knows we're here, of course, but she can't be certain we're after her. Still, turning that searchlight on was a sort of give-away. If she really does go inside it's just because she's afraid of her fuel giving out. We'd better anchor as far out as we can and keep our eyes open until daylight comes."

"She couldn't get gas before morning, I guess," said Joe. "Looks to me as if, if she *is* the *Follow Me*, they've run themselves into a trap!"

"Hope so, I'm sure," said Wink Wheeler. "If we've caught her we've certainly been lucky, fellows!"

"Don't count your chickens until they're hatched," advised Ossie. "Maybe she isn't the *Follow Me* at all."

"I can't see her light now," called Phil from the bow. "Hold on, there's a green light, I think! No, I guess I was wrong. Can't see anything now, Steve. Can you?"

"No, she's turned and run inside back of the breakwater. Keep your ears and eyes open for that whistling buoy, Phil. I want to pass it to port."

"It's pretty near. There it is now! Look!"

"I've got it! All right. Now it's straight for the white beacon." Steve sighed relievedly. "No use hurrying any longer, I guess." He eased the throttle back and the *Adventurer* slowed her pace. "Have a look at the chart, Harry. Isn't there a buoy near the end of the breakwater?"

"Yes, a red spar buoy."

"What's the depth just inside?"

"Four fathoms, shoaling to one."

"Good enough. We'll drop anchor just around the breakwater and train the searchlight across the channel. I don't believe, though, they intend to run out again before morning. All I'm afraid of is that they swung off when darkness came and are sneaking around the Cape."

"I'll bet anything we'll find her at anchor when daylight comes," replied Harry. "She had only enough gas for seventy miles, and she's gone about sixty at top speed. We've got her, Steve. Don't you worry."

"Hope so. Get your bow anchor ready, Han, and stand by to heave. When you let go make as little noise as you can. I'm going to turn the lights out, fellows, so don't go messing about or you may walk overboard. Switch them all off below, Ossie, will you? If those chaps have anchored just inside the breakwater there's no sense in letting them know that this is the *Adventurer*. Got your anchor ready, Han?"

"Ay, ay, sir!"

"All right. Don't let your windlass rattle. Keep quiet, fellows." Suddenly all the lights on deck save that in the binnacle went out, leaving the boat in darkness. Nearby the red flash of the lighthouse glowed periodically, while, ahead, shone the white beacon. In silence the *Adventurer* drew nearer and nearer to the latter, put it abeam and then swung to starboard. "Let her go, Han," called Steve softly. Those on the bridge deck heard the faint splash of the hundred-pound navy anchor as it struck the water. Han crept back and swung himself down to the bridge.

"All fast, sir," he reported.

Somewhere in the darkness at the head of the harbour, where tiny pin-pricks of light twinkled, a town clock struck two.

CHAPTER XII

WHAT STEVE SAW

Waiting was weary work after that. It was two hours and a half to sunrise and, since two of their number were sufficient to keep watch, the others presently went below and napped. Steve and Bert Alley remained on deck. Steve, although he perhaps needed sleep more than anyone, refused to trust other eyes than his own, and while darkness lasted he watched the white path cast across the water by the *Adventurer's* searchlight. But darkness and silence held until shortly after four, when the eastern sky began to lighten. The next half-hour passed more slowly than any that had gone before. Gradually their range of vision enlarged, and Steve, peering into the greyness, drew Bert's attention to a darker hulk that lay a few hundred yards up the harbour. They watched it anxiously as the light increased. That it was a boat of about the size of the *Follow Me* and that is was painted dark became more and more apparent. Then, quite suddenly, a ray of rosy light shot up beyond Eastern Point and the neighbouring motor-boat lay revealed. Steve sighed his disappointment. She was not the *Follow Me* after all, but a battered, black-hulled power-boat used for gill-netting.

One by one, as the light strengthened, the others stumbled on deck, yawning and rubbing their sleepy eyes. The *Adventurer* was anchored more than a mile from the inner harbour, and between her and Ten Pound Island lay a big, rusty-red salt bark, high out of water, and five fishing schooners. But these, aside from the disreputable little gill-netter, were all the craft that met their gaze.

RALPH HENRY BARBOUR

"Either," said Steve wearily, "she never came in at all or she's up in the inner harbour. I'll wager she didn't get out again last night. We'll go up and mosey around, I guess. Ossie, how about some coffee?"

"I'll make some, Steve. Guess we'd better have an early breakfast too."

"It can't be too early to suit me," murmured Bert Alley, as he dragged his feet down the companion way and toppled onto a berth. The *Adventurer* weighed anchor and in the first flush of a glorious Summer dawn, chugged warily up the still harbour. She kept toward the eastern shore and the boys swept every pier and cove with sharp eyes. Then Rocky Neck turned back them and they picked a cautious way over sunken rocks to the entrance of the inner harbour. By this time it was broad daylight and their task was made easier. Still, as the inner harbour was nearly a mile long and a good half-mile wide, and indented with numerous coves, the search was long. They nosed in and out of slips, circled basins and ran down a dozen false clues supplied by sailors on the fishing schooners that lined the wharves. And, at seven o'clock they had to acknowledge defeat. The *Follow Me* was most surely not in Gloucester Harbour. Nor, for that matter, was there a cabin-cruiser that resembled her in any way. It was the latter fact that puzzled them, for they had somehow become convinced that the darkened craft that had led them past the breakwater last night was, if not the *Follow Me*, at least a boat of her size. "And," said Harry Corwin, "we know that that boat did come in here, for we saw her light disappear behind the breakwater. Let's look around again."

"If she came in for gasoline," said Phil, "we might find out whether she got it. There can't be many places where she could fill her tanks." The *Adventurer* was slowly rounding a point that lay between the cove from which she had just emerged and Western Harbour, and Wink Wheeler, who was sitting on the rail on the starboard side of the deck, gave utterance to an exclamation of surprise and pointed ahead to where a drab-coloured power-boat had suddenly emerged into sight nearly a half-mile away.

"Look at that!" he cried.

"That's not the *Follow Me*, you idiot," said Joe.

"No, but where'd she come from?" demanded Wink.

For a moment the boys stared and then Steve leaned quickly over the chart. "By Jiminy!" he muttered. "There's a way out there. Look, fellows! See where it says 'Drawbridge'? Evidently you can get through there into the Squam River, and the river takes you out into Ipswich Bay! It's dollars to doughnuts that's where they took the *Follow Me*!" Steve drew down the throttle and the cruiser lunged forward in response. "We'll have a look, anyway," he said. "It was stupid of me not to have noticed that on the chart, but it's hardly big enough to be seen."

Straight for the beach at the curve of the wide cove sped the *Adventurer*, her nose set for the drawbridge that showed against the blue sky. As they got closer an outlet showed clear, a narrow space between the bridge masonry, with a strong current coming through from the further side.

"Gee, it doesn't look very big," said Joe. "And how about head-room, Steve?"

"Room enough," was the answer, as the *Adventurer* slowed down. "They'll raise the draw if we whistle, I suppose, but we don't need to."

"We'll scrape our funnel, as sure as shooting!" cried Perry as the cruiser neared the bridge.

"We'll miss by two feet," answered Steve untroubledly.

They held their breaths and watched nervously as the shadow of the bridge fell across the boat. Then, with the sound of the engine and exhaust echoing loudly, the cruiser dug her nose into the out-running tide and shot safely through to emerge into a narrow canal that stretched straight ahead before them until it joined the river. They breathed easier as the bridge was left behind. Once in the river it was necessary to go cautiously and watch the channel buoys, for the chart showed a depth of only four feet at low tide for the first mile and a half. If they had not all been so absorbed in the fate and recovery of the *Follow Me* they would have enjoyed that journey down the Squam River immensely, for it was a beautiful stream, quiet and tranquil in the morning sunlight. Summer camps and cottages dotted the shores and green hills hemmed it in. They had breakfast on the way, eating it for the most part on deck. Now and then the *Adventurer* paused while they examined a motor-boat moored in some cove.

"There's one thing certain," said Steve. "Those folks couldn't have brought the *Follow Me* through here in the dark. If they did come through that cut last night they anchored and waited for light. Keep a watch for gasoline stations, fellows."

They found the first one at Annisquam, near where the yacht club pier stuck out into the channel. Steve sidled the *Adventurer* up to a landing and, while Han held her with the hook, made inquiry of a grizzled man in faded blue jumpers.

"We're looking for a motor-boat called the *Follow Me*," he explained. "Have you seen her?"

The man shook his head. "What was she like?" he asked.

Steve described her, aided by Harry Corwin, and the man pushed his old straw hat back, and rubbed his forehead reflectively. Finally: "There was a launch answerin' to that description stopped here about" - he gazed at the sun - "about two hours ago, I cal'ate. She was black, but she didn't have no name on her so far as I could see. I sold 'em thirty gallons o' gas an' they went on out toward the bar."

"Who was on her?" asked Steve quickly.

"Two or three men I never seen before. Three, I cal'ate there was. She wasn't here very long. They come up to the house an' got me up from the breakfast table. Said they was in a hurry. Come to think on it, boys, I believe they'd painted the name out on the stern. They ain't stolen her, have they?"

"That's just what they have done," answered Steve. "Shove off, Han! Thank you, sir. About two hours ago, you say?"

"Might be a little less than two hours. Well, I hope you get her. I didn't much like the looks of the fellers aboard her."

"Where do you think they'd take her?" called Joe as the boat swung her stern around.

"I dunno. They might switch around into the Essex River, or they might take her in Ipswich way, or they might head straight for Newburyport. If they wanted to hide her I cal'ate they might run in behind Plum Island somewheres."

"Sounds pretty hopeless," said Steve as the *Adventurer* took up her way again. "Look at this chart and see all the places she *might* be, will you? It's a regular what-do-you-call-it - labyrinth!"

"It certainly is," agreed Joe. "And there's a lot of shallows about here, too. Where's this Plum Island he spoke of?"

Steve pointed it out, a seven-mile stretch of sand behind which emptied four or five small rivers. "Shall we try it?" he asked.

"Might as well be thorough," Joe replied. "What do you say, Harry?"

"I say yes. Seems to me they'd be mighty likely to slide into some such place if only to paint a new name on."

"We'll have a look then," agreed Steve. The *Adventurer* dipped her way across Squam Bar and Steve swung the wheel. "Southeast, one-fourth south," he muttered, looking from the chart to compass. "Watch for a black spar buoy off the light-house. If they took the *Follow Me* into Essex Bay, though, we're running right away from her."

To port, the sand dunes shone dazzlingly in the sunlight and a long stretch of snow-white beach kept pace with them as they made for the entrance to Plum Island Sound. Several boats, sailing and power craft, had been sighted, but nothing that looked in the least like the *Follow Me*. The sun climbed into a hazy blue sky and the day grew hot in spite of the light westerly breeze. Steve picked up his buoys, a black and then two red, and swung the cruiser in toward the mouth of the Ipswich River. The chart showed feet instead of fathoms in places and Steve slowed down cautiously until they were in the channel. They left Ipswich Light on the port beam and kept on past the river mouth and into the sound.

"What happens," asked Harry Corwin, looking at the chart over Steve's shoulder, "when there aren't any soundings shown?"

"Just what I was wondering myself," replied the navigator. "It doesn't tell you anything after you pass that last red spar buoy. Still, with those two rivers coming in beyond up there, there must be enough water for us if we can find it. I've about arrived at the conclusion that the *Follow Me* was mighty well named, Harry. We've been following her for twelve hours, pretty near, and as things look now we'll be still following her a week from Christmas!"

"I suppose," sighed the captain of the lost boat, "that what we should have done was report it to the police and stayed right where we were. Dad's going to be somewhat peeved if we lose that boat."

"I thought she belonged to you and Tom," said Wink Wheeler.

"So she does, but dad gave her to us and he's rather fond of her himself."

"Well, it's too bad," Wink answered, "but I don't believe we'll ever find her now. It's like looking for a needle in a haystack, this sort of thing. We don't even know for sure that she isn't down around New York somewhere by this time!"

"Yes, we do," said Steve quietly.

"We do? How do we?"

"Because I'm looking at her," was the reply. Steve nodded ahead and pushed back the throttle. "If that isn't the *Follow Me* I'll - I'll eat her!"

CHAPTER XIII

BULLETS FLY

A half-mile or so beyond a black cruiser lay at anchor at the mouth of a cove on the island side of the sound. She was broadside-to and one look at her was enough for Harry Corwin. "It is!" he cried. "We've got her, fellows!"

"Not yet," warned Phil as the fellows clustered from all parts of the boat. "That's her, but how are we going to get her back? Hadn't we better stop here, Steve, and decide what to do? Those men aren't going to give her up just for the asking, I guess."

"Right," agreed Steve. "Bow anchor, Han! Let her go as soon as you're ready. Now then, fellows, let's think what's to be done." The *Adventurer* pulled at the anchor line with her nose, found further progress stopped and slowly began to swing around with the tide. "There are three of them at least, according to the gasoline chap back there, and there are twelve of us, but if they have guns -"

"We've got two revolvers," said Perry eagerly. "Shall I get them, Steve?"

"Yes, fetch them up here, but we don't want to use them unless in self-defence. Don't forget the cartridges, Perry. Now suppose we mosey up to where we can talk to them, fellows."

"That's the ticket , " agreed Wink Wheeler. "If they get to

acting ugly, why, I guess there are enough of us to handle them. I think the best way is to beat it right up there and tell them to hand the boat over."

"And if they decline?" inquired Phil.

"Go in and take it!"

"And, as like as not, get shot full of holes! No, thanks!" This from "Brownie."

"How would it do for some of us to land and keep out of sight and come around back of them?" asked Cas Temple.

"What are we going to do with them if we catch them?" Tom Corwin wanted to know. "Take them back and hand them over to the police?"

"I don't believe they'll let us catch them," answered Phil. "Either they'll take to that small boat they've got astern there or they'll try to make a dash past us."

"Much good that would do them!" Harry shrugged his shoulders. "The *Adventurer* can sail all around our boat."

"We're not getting anywhere," observed Steve, who had been all the while watching the other craft attentively. "And they've seen us at last, for they're looking over the top of the cabin."

"Well, let's do something," said Perry, who was back with the two revolvers and as many boxes of cartridges. "Can they go the other way or do they have to pass us to get out of this place, Steve?"

"They can go the other way for about five miles according to the chart, but they can't get out. There's a bridge there. And, anyway, I guess it's only navigable for small boats at high tide. Perry, for the love of lemons , drop those things and let them alone."

"They aren't loaded," said Perry, injuredly.

"That's the kind that always blow your head off. Well, what's the decision, fellows?"

Everyone talked at once for a minute, and, at last, Phil said: "Why not do the natural thing and ask for our boat? Why let them think that we expect trouble? Perhaps when they see that the game's up they'll give in sensibly."

"That's the idea," agreed Harry and most of the rest. "Let's breeze right up to them and talk big."

"We'll never get the *Follow Me* by lying here, anyway," said Steve, turning to the wheel. "Get your anchor up, Han. Give him a hand, someone. Wink, open a box of those cartridges and load the revolvers, will you? But keep them out of Perry's way! All right now. Settle down, fellows, and we'll try a bluff."

The *Adventurer* went on and the distance between the two boats lessened rapidly. They could see two men watching them over the top of the cabin, but there was no sign of alarm visible aboard the *Follow Me*. When the *Adventurer* was almost opposite the black cruiser Steve threw out the clutch, turned the wheel and let her run shoreward. "We're getting out of the channel," he said to Harry. "Watch for sand-bars." He slipped the clutch in again and again disengaged it. The two boats were some twenty yards apart now and the men on the *Follow Me* were observing the newcomers unblinkingly from the cockpit.

Steve leaned over the rail and sent a hail across. "*Follow Me*, ahoy!" he called. "We'll trouble you for that boat, please."

For a moment there was no answer. Then one of the two men in sight moved forward and drawled: "Speaking to us, are you? What was it you said?"

"I said we'd trouble you for that boat," repeated Steve. "It happens to belong to us, you see."

"This boat?"

"That identical boat."

"Belongs to you!"

"You've got it."

"That's a good joke, friend. We've owned this boat three years. Where do you come in?"

"She's the *Follow Me*, even if you have painted her name out, and you took her from her anchorage in Plymouth Harbour last night. What's the use of throwing a fool bluff like that?"

The man laughed hoarsely and his companion joined him. "Run away, kids!" he said finally. "You're crazy with the heat. This boat's the *Esmeralda*, of Providence, and she belongs to me and this feller. What do you mean, took her? Callin' me a thief, are you?"

"I'm not taking the trouble to. If you know what's good for you you'll dig out of there and do it quick."

"Is that so?" drawled the man. "Well, ain't that nice? An' supposin' it don't suit me to hand over my boat to you? Then what you goin' to do?"

"Take her," answered Steve quietly. "There are twelve of us here and we've followed you all the way from Plymouth, and we aren't likely to let you bluff us off now. Come on, now, what do you say?"

"Come on and take her, kids!" was the answer. "We're scared to death!" The men thought that extremely funny, and laughed a lot over it. Just then, Steve, leaning outboard over the railing, felt someone tug at his arm.

"Look at the middle port, Steve," whispered Phil.

Steve looked. The nearer side of the *Follow Me* was in shadow, but a quivering beam of sunlight, reflected from the surface of the water, glinted on the muzzle of a revolver held just inside the open port.

"Every fellow under cover," said Steve quietly. "That means you, too, Joe. Duck! They've got a gun trained on us. Who's the best shot here?"

"Wink," answered Joe.

"Give him one of the revolvers. Are you there, Wink?"

"Yes," answered the other from the forward companion way.

"Get a bead on that middle port. You'll see a gun sticking through there. Don't shoot unless they shoot first. Better go into the other cabin. There's no harm in letting them see you, but don't keep your head exposed. Someone hand me that other revolver."

On the other boat Steve's silence was accepted as a confession of indecision and a jeering laugh came across the water. The *Adventurer* was drifting toward the shore now, and Steve turned and slipped the clutch into reverse and churned back a few yards. Then he faced the men again.

"You can't get away with it, you know," he said untroubledly. "We can stay here as long as you can. If you run we'll follow you, and at the first port we'll hand you over to the authorities. You've only got thirty gallons of gas and that won't take you far. If you have any sense you'll pile into your tender and light out while you've got a good chance."

It was evident that those on the stolen boat had glimpsed Wink's revolver, for one of the men leaned toward his companion and spoke in low tones and their eyes sought the port. After a moment the spokesman replied placatingly. "Maybe you're right, Sport. Guess you've got us this time. But this ain't any place to go ashore. Tell you what we'll do. We'll run her back to Gloucester and hand her over to you there. That's fair, ain't it?"

"It doesn't listen well," answered Steve. "You land on the other side there and you'll only have to walk a few miles to a train."

"Yeah, walk about six miles across sand dunes in a sun hot enough to blister you! Nothin' doin', Sport. Take it or leave it."

"Leave it, thanks."

For answer one of the men climbed to the cabin roof and went forward. "He's going to pull up anchor," warned Joe, peering over the rail. Steve's voice rang out sharply:

"If you touch that cable we'll shoot!"

The man paused, stared across doubtfully and went on.

"Can you hear me, Wink?" asked Steve softly.

"Yes," came from the after cabin.

"If he lays a hand on the anchor cable, shoot, but shoot wide."

"All right, Steve!"

"Say," called the man in the cockpit, "don't you start nothin', because we got you covered. If there's any shootin' you'll get the worst of it."

The man forward dropped to a knee, his gaze turned warily toward the enemy, and took hold of the anchor cable. As he did so Steve whipped his revolver into sight and flattened himself against the bulkhead. A sharp report broke the silence and a bullet sang its way across the *Follow Me's* bow. The man dropped the rope and sprang back along the roof to tumble frightenedly into the cockpit. From the cabin of the *Adventurer* floated up the acrid smoke of Wink's revolver. The man at the stern of the other boat had instantly disappeared.

"Look out," shouted Perry from the forward cabin. "They're going to shoot from the ports! Come down from there, Steve!"

But Steve's hand was on the clutch and, as the *Adventurer* began to go astern, his other hand turned the spokes of the wheel and the cruiser's bow came slowly around toward the *Follow Me.* "Come up here, Wink," he called, and then: "Put that hatch up all the way and keep behind it," he added as Wink slipped to his side. "Can you get them from there?"

"Fine!" answered the other cheerfully.

"I'll try to keep her bow-on. Careful not to kill anyone, old man. Shoot for their arms."

"How can I when they're out of sight down there?" Wink complained. "All I can do is shoot for the ports."

"Don't shoot at all unless you have to," Steve cautioned. "We don't want to knock any more splinters off her than necessary."

"We're too near, Steve. The deck's getting in the way."

"I'll back her off." The *Adventurer* retreated until Wink, his elbow resting on the closed cover of the chart-box, could train his revolver on the *Follow Me's* ports. Several of the others emerged from the cabins and huddled from sight on the deck.

"What's the next act, Steve?" inquired Phil.

Steve shook his head. "I'm wondering," he answered. "About all we can do is keep them from running away until they talk sense."

"Why not let them run? We can go faster than they can."

"I'm afraid of tricks," responded Steve. "I don't know these waters, and I suspect that they do. They might manage to give us the slip as they did last night. I guess when they find they can't get away they'll come to terms." Steve raised his head cautiously above the chart-box on his side and a bullet promptly ploughed through the frame of the open window in front of him and went singing astern.

"Rotten shooting," observed Wink, as Steve ducked to safety. "Shall I give 'em one, Steve?"

Steve hesitated and then shook his head. "What's the use? You'd only plug a hole in the *Follow Me's* cabin. Wait until they show themselves."

"Well, you take care not to show yourself," advised Wink, peering warily past the smoke-stack. "Those murderous pirates are shooting to kill, I guess."

Another shot rang out across the dancing water and a bullet flattened itself against a pipe stanchion. "Guess you'd better put a shot into each of those ports," said Steve. "Maybe they'll keep away from them. Sorry to damage your boat, Harry."

"Bother the damage!" said Harry. "Plug her full of lead if you like!"

Wink's revolver spoke, and: "Bull's-eye," he announced calmly. Another shot followed. "Got that one, too," he muttered. "Can't see the other port from here, Steve. Smoke-stack's in the way. You try it."

Steve tried and missed, the bullet knocking a long splinter from the edge of the cabin roof, and at the same moment a pistol aboard the *Follow Me* barked and Perry, sitting crouched on one of the seats, uttered an exclamation. Phil, beside him, turned anxiously. Perry's face expressed blank amazement as he pushed his right sleeve up and gazed at a wound from which the blood was spurting.

"Gosh," he said awedly, "I'm shot!"

CHAPTER XIV

A RUSE THAT FAILED

"I should think so!" cried Phil. "Come on down and let me fix it."

"What is it?" asked Steve anxiously.

"Perry's hit in the arm. They must have shot along the side, and the bullet glanced from something. Come on, Perry."

"All you fellows get out of here," commanded Steve. "It might happen again, and you're not doing any good here, anyway. The chest's in the bottom locker in our cabin, Phil. Is it bad?"

"Don't think so," was the reply from the companion way. "Only a flesh wound, I guess. I'll look after it."

Steve had forgotten to try a second shot at the port, but Wink again let go at where the glint of a revolver muzzle showed and a cry of pain came across the water.

"Got him!" said Wink.

"You must have," agreed Steve. "I hope you didn't hurt him much."

"Suffering snakes!" ejaculated Wink. "Why shouldn't I hurt him? They potted Perry, didn't they? What are we supposed to do! Lie around here and let them shoot us full of lead and just smile? Why, you pig-headed, solid concrete -"

But Wink's flow of eloquence was interrupted by two shots from the *Follow Me*. There was a tinkling of glass as one of them smashed through the upper frame of the window on Steve's side. The other ploughed into the chart-box. Wink instantly fired back twice, aiming at the two ports he commanded. "Harry's boat will look like a sieve," he chuckled as he broke his revolver and jammed fresh cartridges into it. "Get busy there, Steve!"

For answer Steve's revolver spoke twice and the thud of the bullets came to them. "Got the boat anyway," chuckled Wink. "We can scare 'em even if we can't pot 'em! Better back up a little, Steve. I don't want to bust our flag-pole."

Once more the *Adventurer* increased the distance between her and the adversary, and once more the engine beneath their feet relapsed into a quiet purr as the load was taken off again.

"If it wasn't that we'd bust the *Follow Me*," exclaimed Steve savagely, "I'd ram them! They're knocking our paint off and breaking our glass and raising the dickens!"

Wink glanced across the deck. Steve, his revolver laid on the floor beside him, was knotting a handkerchief about his hand with his teeth. "Hello!" exclaimed Wink. "Did they get you!"

"No, it's only a piece of glass. It's bleeding a bit, that's all." Steve gave a final tug at the knot and seized his revolver again. "I wish they'd show themselves!"

"They probably wish the same of us," laughed Wink. "How long does this keep up? I'm getting hungry!"

"It keeps up until they give in," responded Steve determinedly. "Below there! Tell Ossie to start on the dinner."

"Dinner!" exclaimed Ossie from the aft companion. "Suppose they plugged a bullet into the galley?"

"Don't be an idiot," begged Steve impatiently. "You've got four inches of planking and a pile of rope and a refrigerator and a lot of other stuff between you and the bullets. Get busy and do your bit!"

"All right, Steve. I'd forgotten about the refrigerator. But you can bet I'm not going to leave the door open!" This jest was rewarded with a laugh from the others as Ossie pushed his way past them and dived hurriedly across the deck to the forward companion way. "Pistols and coffee for twelve," he added as he disappeared.

For several minutes there was no further sound or movement aboard the *Follow Me*. "They're probably fixing up the chap who got plugged," opined Wink cheerfully, as he watched the ports. "Wish we had a rifle, Steve. We could get them right through the hull, I guess."

"Yes, and if we had a torpedo we could sink her," said Cas Temple from the hatch. "Suppose they've run out of cartridges, Steve?"

"I don't believe so. I guess they don't think it's worth while wasting what they've got."

A cheering aroma of coffee stole up from the galley and murmurs of satisfaction were heard. Perry, his forearm bandaged neatly and scientifically, crowded his way up the after companion. "Say, Steve, let me have a shot at them, will you?" he begged earnestly. "Just one, Steve, like a good fellow!"

"How's the arm, Perry?"

"Oh, all right, I guess. It hurts a little. Phil's got it so blamed tight that I can't close my fingers. Will you, Steve?"

Steve was denied an answer by a sudden interruption from Wink. "She's moving, Steve!" he cried. "They've started her!"

"But they're anchored!" exclaimed Joe.

"They've cut the line. Probably reached through a port on the other side," said Steve, working quickly at the controls. "It's lucky we didn't have ours down, too!"

The *Follow Me*, gathering headway, pushed for the channel, and the *Adventurer* lunged forward with a mighty splashing of her screw, Steve bringing her head around as fast as he could. "How the dickens are they steering her, Harry?" he demanded, staring in puzzlement at the empty cockpit of the other craft.

"There's an auxiliary wheel forward, in the stateroom. They're coming around, fellows. Get under cover! Steve, you'd better drop!"

The others scuttled for the companion ways, and none too soon, for, as the *Follow Me* swung around into the channel those behind her ports had a clean sweep of the *Adventurer's* bridge deck and a fusillade of shots swept across the forty or fifty yards dividing the boats. Steve and Wink had dropped below the rail, while, in the cabins, the others were taking good care to crouch beneath the level of the ports. Some eight shots were fired, but, although several took effect on various parts of the bridge, the fact that the *Adventurer* was now plunging around in a half-circle at a full twelve miles an hour and the other boat was running at top speed down the channel made accuracy impossible. Neither Steve nor Wink had a chance to reply until it was too late for their shots to be effective. By that time the two cruisers had straightened out on the course and the chase had begun.

Harry Corwin was entrusted with Steve's revolver and, standing on the dining table set from locker to locker across the galley, he could thrust head and shoulders through the hatch. But the cockpit of the *Follow Me* remained empty and the entrance to the cabin was closed. Wink, his revolver ready, had returned to his post and watched grimly while the *Adventurer*, her engine fairly humming, slowly wore down the distance that separated her from the enemy.

"They're certainly getting some speed out of her," called Wink admiringly. The rest of the company had returned to the bridge and were watching eagerly. Tom Corwin, who had remained unaffected by the potting of the *Follow Me's* hull, was fighting mad now because the thieves had lost the bow anchor, and sputtered wrathfully as he gazed over Steve's shoulder. "If I was Harry I'd put a bullet through that door," he muttered. "I wish someone would let me have a shot at them!"

"You couldn't hit her at this distance, with the boats swinging," said Steve. "Wonder why it doesn't occur to them to cut away that tender. It's taking a mile off their speed."

"Afraid of getting hit, I guess," replied Joe.

"It doesn't seem to me that we're gaining very fast."

"We're not, but we're gaining fast enough. Hello!" The *Follow Me*, having approached the end of the island, had turned her nose to port straight for the end of the beach. "How much does she draw, Tom?"

"Two feet and a half; same as this."

"And the chart shows two feet of water there at low tide!" exclaimed Steve. "And it's nearly dead low now, I guess. She's taking a chance, all right!"

The channel ran straight ahead, close to the shore of the mainland, and if the *Follow Me's* exploit proved successful she was due to increase her dwindling lead by a good mile unless the *Adventurer* accepted the challenge and followed her example. For a minute Steve hesitated. Then: "If she can do it, we can," he muttered, and slowly turned the wheel, his eyes darting to the chart. "No depth shown here," he said. "Two feet further along. Then four and seven. If we can get to the point of sand there we're all right."

They watched the *Follow Me* breathlessly. She was dancing almost in the breakers now and for a long moment it seemed that she would surely pile herself on the spit that ran seaward from the end of the island. But she got by safely and the *Adventurer* plunged after her. There were strained faces on the bridge deck then and Ossie was seen to lay a tentative hand on the cushion of the nearer seat. Steve, with grim countenance, kept his eyes on the rollers, trying his best to follow in the wake of the other boat. Here and there white water hinted at shoals and it was between two of these that the *Follow Me* had gone. Steve eased the wheel and slowed the engine a trifle and the *Adventurer*, rocking in the long swells that were breaking on the beach hardly more than a stone-throw to port, went on. Steve was in the act of breathing a long sigh of relief when there came a jar that threw several of the boys off their balance and brought cries of consternation to their lips. For one horrid moment the *Adventurer* hung with her propeller churning the sand, and then shook herself free and lunged forward again.

Shouts of relief went up and a smile of triumph came to Steve's face as he pulled her back into the course and slipped into deeper water. The *Follow Me* was still a good eighth of a mile ahead and swinging northward around the curve of beach. "They're going to make for Newburyport," said Steve. "Watch them try to get me into trouble now, Joe."

"How do you mean?"

"They're keeping in close to shore. See? Look on the chart."

"I see twelve little black crosses about there. What do they mean? Oh, I get you. 'Emerson Rocks,' eh? But I don't see them!"

"No, they're sunken. The *Follow Me's* running as near them as she dares, hoping that we'll try to cut the corner more and strike. Those fellows know this coast as I know the inside of my hat! But we'll fool them this time!"

So close to the submerged danger did the *Adventurer* go that Perry, watching over the side, caught a glimpse of a dark mass under the green water. Then the chase straightened out once more and Steve drew the throttle wide, experimented with the spark for a moment and sent the white cruiser surging along in pursuit. There could be no doubt as to the outcome of the race. It was only a question of time. The thieves had staked all on the attempt to elude the *Adventurer* in the shallows, and now they were doomed to open water, for Plum Island ran straight and unbroken for seven miles, and not until the entrance to Newburyport Harbour was reached was there the smallest chance to slip out of sight.

Ossie announced that dinner would be ready in a few minutes, but no one paid any attention. Every eye was fixed on the *Follow Me*, which, dead ahead, was scurrying along at a rate which Tom, who had thought he knew the engine thoroughly, marvelled at. But the distance was shortening between pursued and pursuer. Off the life-saving station the fleeing craft was scarcely a hundred yards in advance, and it became more and more certain that the boats would be on even terms long before the seven-mile stretch was half traversed.

Wink went below and summoned Harry Corwin down from his perch, much to the relief of Ossie, whose preparations for dinner had not been made easier by having to dive under the table every time he sought the ice-chest, and posted him at a port in the forward cabin. "If they won't give up," he explained, "we'll have to go on plugging them. I'll take it in the other cabin. Better fire first from one port then from another. That'll keep them guessing. It's just as well for them not to know that we've got only two pieces of artillery!"

"All right," said Harry, "but there's no use staying here now, is there? There's nothing in sight but a sea-gull!"

"No, but be ready when we get abreast, Harry. I think that

gun pulls to the right a little. You might watch it."

Wink returned to the deck, followed by Harry as far as the companion, and looked forward at the *Follow Me*. Since he had gone below the positions of the boats had altered noticeably, and now, had he wished, he might easily have put a bullet through the mahogany door beyond the cockpit. Steve was bearing seaward a little, intending to run up on the starboard side of the black cruiser.

"I'll bet they're doing a whole lot of thinking about now," said "Brownie." "Guess I'll go down and sit on the floor again. They'll be able to plug us in another minute or so."

"You'd all better beat it," said Steve. "If the bullets begin to fly again someone will get hurt."

Slowly but certainly the bow of the *Adventurer* crept up on the *Follow Me's* stern. Some sixty feet of water divided them. Beyond the black cruiser lay the long yellow beach, dazzling in the noonday sunlight. Suddenly the *Follow Me's* bow turned straight for the breakers and Steve gave a cry.

CHAPTER XV

SURRENDER

"They're going to run her ashore!" shouted Steve.

He slid out the clutch, throttled down the engine and swung the boat's nose to starboard as the others piled back to the deck. The *Adventurer* swept around in a long circle while the *Follow Me*, churning the shoaling water into white froth, ran straight for the shore.

"Gosh, what a mess!" groaned Harry Corwin. "We'll never get her off there!"

Steve made no answer, nor did the others. They were all watching that wild rush of the black cruiser. On and on she went, rising and falling with the gentle swells, until it looked as though she must surely be churning the sand with her hurrying screw. Suddenly the cabin doors flew open and three men, one hatless and with a white towel bound around his head, leaped out and scampered along the roof to the bow. Wink raised his revolver, but Steve pulled his arm down.

"Don't!" he said. "Let them go if they will."

At that instant the *Follow Me* faltered, stopped, and went on again for another yard or so as a breaking wave rushed under her keel, and then rolled over to starboard and subsided so, her propeller still beating and her stern slowly working around. Into the two feet of water dropped the trio on the bow and, keeping the *Follow Me* between them and the enemy, scuttled

RALPH HENRY BARBOUR

to land, and then, once on the hard sand, ran as hard as their legs would take them up the beach to the north. Wink sent one shot hurtling after them, just, as he explained afterwards, to encourage them, and Steve, having cautiously edged the *Adventurer* as near shore as he dared, gave his orders hurriedly.

"Get the big cable from the rope locker, Han," he directed. "Joe, you and Harry jump into the tender and stand by here. When you get the cable pull in to the *Follow Me* and make it fast to the stern cleat. Tom, you'd better go along, too. Put your engine into reverse and try to back off. The tide's still running out and if we don't get her off now we'll have a hard time later. I'll pull on the stern and you jockey her with her own power. I think we can do it. Now then, Han, give me that. Here, take this end forward and make it fast around the cleat. Pass it outside that stanchion, you chump! Catch, Harry! All right! Get a move on, fellows!"

Off plugged the tender, Joe bending furiously at the short oars, the big cable paying out astern. A minute or two later they were tumbling aboard the *Follow Me*, Tom to dart below to the engine, Harry to make fast their end of the line and Joe to look after the tender. Then Harry waved a hand and shouted, and the *Adventurer*, which had been going slowly astern, taking up the slack of the cable, settled to her task. The big rope tightened, throwing a spray of water into the sunlight along its length, strained and creaked and the *Follow Me's* propeller, reversed, did its part. There was an anxious two minutes. Very grudgingly the black cruiser's stern came around. Steve drew the *Adventurer's* throttle down a couple of notches. The *Follow Me* gave up her notion of spending her declining years on the sands of Plum Island and slowly backed away. A shout of delight arose from a dozen throats as, with the water once more under her she bobbed sedately to an even keel and followed the tug of the big hawser.

A quarter of an hour later the two boats continued their way up the shore, the *Follow Me* poorer by one eighty-pound anchor and richer by one cedar dingey which the six boys aboard seriously suspected of having been stolen. They ate dinner at half-past two, anchored on Joppa Flats, the two crews once more assembled around and about the *Adventurer's* hospitable board, and as they ate, very hungrily and quite happily, they discussed the day's adventure.

The *Follow Me* showed numerous signs of Steve's and Wink's marksmanship, both outside and in, but there was no damage that nails and hammer, paint and putty wouldn't repair. The stolen boat's larder was sadly depleted and, as Tom said disgustedly, the cabin looked as though a dozen pigs had lived in it a week! But, all in all, the cruiser had come off well. As for the lost anchor, why, as Wink pointed out, the tender would more than buy them a new one. There was some discussion as to their right to dispose of that tender and in the end they agreed that the proper thing to do would be to leave it at Newburyport and mail an advertisement to the Plymouth papers. If the owner claimed the boat he would pay for the advertisement. If he didn't, they would recover it later on their way back down the coast. The *Adventurer*, too, showed numerous scars. One bullet had plugged straight in at one side of the smokestack and out the other, the glass in one window had been shattered to bits and in various other places damage had been wrought. But they had recovered the *Follow Me*, and that, viewing the affair in retrospect, had been something of an achievement. Everyone, even Tom by now, was more than satisfied at the outcome of their first real adventure. Dinner, delayed as it was and none too palatable by reason of having been prepared for a much earlier hour, was a merry meal.

After it was over they went on up to Newburyport, found a berth and set out to look for a yard where they could have the two cruisers patched. Repairs kept them there two days, and then, having acquired a new anchor for the *Follow Me* and left the extra dingey in safe storage, the Adventure Club set forth once more in the early hours of a drizzly morning.

They passed the Isles of Shoals before nine and in the middle of the forenoon Steve pointed through the haze to where an indistinct blot against the sky line proclaimed Boon Island. After that the cruisers kept well toward shore, for, although the drizzle had stopped, the navigators feared that a fog might take its place, and that one experience in Vineyard Sound had been sufficient to last them for the balance of the cruise. Off Cape Porpoise the boats found rough seas and the crew of the *Follow Me* were secretly delighted to observe that the smaller craft made much easier going. The *Adventurer* seemed to be having a thoroughly good time, for she kicked up her heels and waved her nose and fairly rolled in merriment as the seas came sliding under her quarter. The bridge deck was a damp place until both side curtains were lowered and laced to the rails and stanchions. Poor Joe stood it as long as he could, getting paler and paler and sitting, hands in pockets, gazing fixedly at the brass kickplate at the top of the forward companion way, about the only thing in his range of vision that was fairly steady, and at intervals lurching below with an assumption of carelessness that deceived nobody, to dose himself with his sea-sickness remedy. That remedy, however, failed him, and it was not very long before the Chief Engineer was conspicuous on the bridge by his absence, while those who listened could hear at intervals a low moaning sound proceeding from the after cabin. But Joe was not the only one aboard the *Adventurer* who suffered qualms of uneasiness, although he alone gave up the struggle. Both Perry and Han showed pale countenances and looked big-eyed and pathetic. Neither displayed the least interest in dinner, while Joe, when cruelly summoned by Ossie, only groaned lugubriously and turned his pallid face to the wall. At two o'clock the sun broke through and dyed the sea a wonderful green, and the *Adventurer* began to meet other boats. As she left Scarboro Beach on her port beam and began to nose in toward Peak's Island the sea calmed and by the time the cruiser was ready to drop her anchor in Portland harbour, Joe, albeit still rather greenish, had pulled himself back to deck to gaze approvingly at the shore.

A week went by during which the Adventure Club, one and all, had a glorious time without anything that in the least resembled adventure. They spent a whole day in Portland -

spent, also, a deal of money there replenishing an utterly exhausted galley - and then, to use Perry's inelegant phrase, "bummed around" Casco Bay for three days more. Joe fell in love with more islands during that time than he had known existed. "I've always wanted to own an island," he would explain, "and that's the very island. Let's go ashore, Steve, and look around."

Steve humoured him several times, until the others complained that they were getting tired of stopping at every bunch of rocks on the Maine Coast, and pointed out, besides, that, as Perry had owned to having but nine dollars in his pocket just a few days before, it wasn't at all likely that he would find an island within his means. After exhausting the interest of Casco Bay the two boats ran further up the shore and spent another forty-eight hours at Camden. Steve had friends there and the whole tribe of mariners were invited to dinners and luncheons and found that "home cooking" was all that it was popularly believed to be. Ossie had a most perfect time during those two days.

"Nothing to cook but breakfast," he said ecstatically, "and real food the other two meals! Gee, but it's fine to eat something some other poor duffer has cooked! Say, Joe, what is it that pigs have that kills them off in bunches: sort of a - an epidemic?"

"Hog cholera," hazarded Joe. "Aren't you feeling well, Ossie?"

"Well, I wish they'd all have it," said Ossie devoutly. "I'm so plumb sick of cooking bacon!"

The rest agreed, away from Ossie's hearing, that it was a very fortunate thing that the period of eating ashore had arrived when it did, for Ossie had been showing symptoms of mutiny of late and his cooking had noticeably fallen off. "He was due to strike in another few days," said Han. "Then someone else would have had to take the job, and we would all have starved to death."

"In the absence of the cook," observed Perry gravely, "the job falls to the crew."

"No, sir, to the second mate," corrected Han. "Isn't that so, Joe?"

"I'm not sure. The only thing I am sure of is that - um - it doesn't fall to the chief engineer."

"I should say not!" retorted Perry. "Think of eating food flavoured with engine oil!"

"Couldn't be any worse than pudding flavoured with onion extract," chuckled Joe, referring to a viand prepared by Ossie while at Newburyport. Ossie had meant to put in a spoonful of vanilla, but the two bottles looked so much alike -

The pudding was never eaten, unless the fish consumed it, and the mention of it still caused Ossie great pain and humiliation.

They went into the water every morning before breakfast, lived almost every minute in the open air - for even at night the wide-open ports and doors made the cabins like sleeping porches - ate heartily, got enough exercise to keep them lean and hungry and became tanned with sun and wind to the colour of light mahogany. Khaki trousers, sleeveless shirts and rubber-soled canvas shoes made up their ordinary attire, although for shore visits they "dolled up" remarkably. Those early morning baths were fine appetisers, as will be understood by the reader who has had experience of the water along the Maine coast, and the number of eggs and slices of crisp bacon that came off the alcohol stove would sound like a fairy tale if told. At Camden the two cruisers lay side by side, with just enough room between to allow them to swing, and by keeping the tenders alongside the gangways it was only a momentary task to ferry from one boat to the other. In consequence the two crews mingled a good deal and it was no unusual thing for one breakfast table to be thronged while the other was half empty of a morning. When the boys got tired of swimming they simply climbed over the rail of the nearer craft and, after partly drying themselves, went down to breakfast. As getting dry was a somewhat perfunctory proceeding, the linoleum in the forward cabin was covered with pools of salt water by the time the last platter of bacon and eggs was empty.

Many friends were made and the boys spent more time on shore than aboard. There was tennis to be played, for one thing, and Phil, Steve and Joe were all dabsters at that game. And then there was a big, freckle-faced youth named Globbins who spent most of his waking hours in the driver's seat of a high-powered roadster automobile and who ran the fellows many miles over the roads and was never, seemingly, more contented than when every available inch of the car was occupied. Its normal capacity was three, but by careful packing it was possible to get seven in, on or about it. In return, Globbins was entertained aboard the *Adventurer* and given a thirty-mile cruise one evening, but it was easy to see that he wasn't really enjoying himself and that his hands fairly ached for the feel of that corrugated wheel of the roadster. They had such a jolly time at Camden that they promised faithfully to stop there again on the return voyage, and really meant to keep the promise when they chugged out of the harbour one crisp morning and turned the cruisers' bows eastward for the run across Penobscot Bay.

They lazed that day, for, as Steve said, it was too fine to hurry. Dinner was eaten with the two boats side by side, with only fenders between, in a fairy pool. They found the place quite by accident when exploring the shore of an island whose name they are to this day ignorant of. There was an entrance to the tiny bay through which a schooner might barely have scraped her way. Beyond the mouth lay a wonder land. The pool was as round as a dish and its water the bluest they had ever seen. Straight across from the entrance a cliff of granite towered for a hundred feet or more, its tree-clad summit almost leaning over the boats at anchor. Its face was clothed with vines and dwarf evergreens and birches. On the other encircling shores of the pool tumbled boulders hung over the blue depths and were reflected so clearly that, looking down, one received the same impression of air and space as when lying on one's back staring into the sky. There never were such reflections, they declared. No one came to disturb them, and only the songs and chirpings of birds and the sleepy sigh of the faint breeze in the boughs broke the silence. Green and blue was that fairyland, warm with the sun and redolent of the sea and the sappy fragrance of sun-bathed foliage.

They ate dinner on the decks, the two boats snuggled so close that it was the easiest thing in the world to pass dishes from one to another. After dinner they lolled in the sunlight and gazed up at the sheer granite bluff or the smiling and cloudless sky and talked lazily or slumbered a little. And finally Wink Wheeler thought of fishing and in a few minutes a half-dozen lines were overboard, and, while the catches were not big, they were fairly frequent, and the question of what they were to have for supper was solved there and then. It was Harry Corwin's idea to stay in the pool overnight and everyone instantly applauded it. Later, a party went ashore and explored, but there were no paths to be found and Nature was jealous of her secrets and they came back without more knowledge of this unknown island than they had had before. They named it Mystery Island and called the little harbour Titania's Mirror, a suggestion from Bert Alley which elicited jibes and a final agreement.

"It's not 'mushy' a bit," said Steve, in Bert's defence. "It's a fine name for the prettiest bit of water any of us ever saw, and you know it. The only trouble with you is that you're afraid someone will laugh at you for being poetical or imaginative. If Bert had suggested calling it Put-In Bay or Simpkins' Cove or something like that you'd have said 'Fine!' and secretly thought him a perfect ass!"

Twilight came early and the still, limpid water of the pool took on all sorts of strange and wonderful hues, like the iridescent surface of a pearl-shell. It grew very still and a little bit eery as the shadows crept over the scene, and it was a relief when Cas

Temple and Bert Alley brought forth their mandolins. I am sorry to say that Titania's Mirror was a bit too thickly inhabited by mosquitoes for comfort, and there were restless turnings and muttered expostulations to be heard for some time after lights were out.

The morning broke radiantly and at half-past six Titania's Mirror was turned into a highly satisfactory bathtub. Brown arms clove the shadowed surface and dripping heads rose and fell as fully half the number set out on a spirited race to the entrance. When almost there they emerged into a flood of pale sunlight, and looking down through the pellucid water they could see the sloping sides of the basin converging like the sides of a bowl. Tragedy was surely the last thing to be thought of amidst such idyllic surroundings, and yet it was hovering very close.

RALPH HENRY BARBOUR

CHAPTER XVI

THE BURGLARS

Wink Wheeler reached the little channel first and gingerly climbed out on a brown ledge that flanked it on one side. Others joined him there to lie panting in the sunlight. Only Joe and Phil kept on and were presently swimming within a short distance of each other well outside. They were both strong rather than fast swimmers, and, although Han frowned slightly as he watched them bob in and out of sight in the long, smooth swells, the others soon turned their attention to Wink's suggestion that they dive from the rock and race around the anchored boats and back again. Wink offered the others a ten-yard start. All save "Brownie" accepted the challenge - "Brownie" was built for comfort rather than speed - and in a moment they were lined up rather unsteadily on the edge of the boulder awaiting the word. Then three bodies launched themselves through the air and the race was on. When the others had taken the first half-dozen strokes after reappearing Wink plunged after them. "Brownie" watched until the foremost swimmer disappeared beyond the boats and then turned his gaze seaward. For a moment he could not find the two venturesome ones, but presently he spied them. They had turned and were coming back straight for the mouth of the little harbour, Phil leading and Joe a dozen yards behind. It looked like a race from the way in which both boys were keeping under and "Brownie" found it more exciting than the other contest. And then, while he watched, something happened, and he sprang to his feet and gazed seaward with wildly beating heart.

Joe had stopped swimming and was on his back with one brown arm held aloft. If he made any outcry "Brownie" failed to hear it, but apparently he had, for Phil was turning now and hurrying back with short, quick strokes. But before he had covered half the distance separating him from the other, the watcher on shore uttered an involuntary cry of alarm. Joe was no longer in sight!

"Brownie" looked despairingly toward the boys in the pool, but the nearest was still a long way from the channel. Confused thoughts of the boats were cast aside and "Brownie" threw himself from the rock, hitting the water like a barrel, and turned into the channel. As he felt the tug of the tide he experienced a revulsion of fright, for he had no stomach for the task ahead of him. "Brownie's" swimming was usually done in safer water than that he was making for. But he tried his best to forget the depths below him and the long swim ahead, to remember only that Joe was in trouble out there and that Phil, probably by now somewhat exhausted, would never be able to bring him to shore unassisted.

The long swells hid the others from him. Once, though, poised for a moment on the round summit of a bank of water, he glimpsed ere he descended into the green valley beyond, a darker spot ahead and so found his direction. He knew better than to tire himself out by desperate strokes. His only hope of getting there and getting back was to conserve his strength. All sorts of thoughts came and went in a strange jumble. Sometimes it seemed that he was making no progress, that the slow waves were bearing him remorselessly back to the cove, or, at least just defeating the strokes of his arms and legs. Breathing became laboured and once a veritable panic seized him and it was all he could do to keep from turning and swimming wildly back toward shore. Instead, though, fighting his fears, he turned on his back for a moment with his round face to the blue breeze-swept sky, and took long, grateful breaths of the sun-sweet air. Above him a grey gull swept in a wide circle, uttering harsh, discordant cries. Then, his panic gone, "Brownie" turned over again and struggled on with renewed

RALPH HENRY BARBOUR

strength and courage. And suddenly, the long swells were behind him and there, but a few yards away, was Phil, Phil very white of face but as calm as ever.

He was swimming slowly on his side, one arm cleaving the water and the other supporting the nearly inert body of Joe. "Here comes 'Brownie,'" the rescuer heard him say cheerfully. "All right now, Joe. We'll get you in in a jiffy! Roll over, 'Brownie,' and get your breath," he added. "We're all right for a minute. That's the trick."

"I'm - a bit - tuckered," gasped "Brownie," as he lay and puffed with outstretched arms.

"Don't blame you," said Phil. "How are you now, Joe?"

"Punk," muttered the other. "Don't you fellows bother too much. If you'll just stay by for a minute or two - I'll be - um - all right, I guess."

"No need to do that," replied Phil quietly. "'Brownie' and I will take you between us. Put a hand on my shoulder. Easy, son! That's it. Now the other on 'Brownie's.' Right you are. Just let yourself float. Ready, 'Brownie?' Don't hurry. Easy does it. We've got an eighth of a mile or so and there's no use getting tired at the start. I guess the tide will help us, though."

There were no more words until the shore was nearly reached. By that time "Brownie" was frankly all-in and Phil was in scarcely better condition. Joe had so far recovered then, however, as to be able to aid weakly with his legs, and before they reached the channel half a dozen eager helpers splashed to their assistance. Anxious questions were showered on them, but only Joe had the breath to answer them.

"I had a cramp," he explained apologetically. "It hit me all of a sudden out there. It was fierce!"

"Legs?" asked Steve.

"No - yes - about everywhere below my shoulders. It seemed to start in my tummy. I got sort of sick all over. Thought - um - thought I was a goner until -"

"All right! Shut up now. Someone give Phil a hand. He's about ready to quit. 'Brownie,' too." Steve and Wink had taken the places of the rescuers and Joe was finishing his journey at top speed. It was no easy task getting him aboard, but they finally accomplished it and hurried him below. "Brownie," too, had to be pushed and pulled over the side, and while Phil got aboard almost unaided he slumped onto a seat and, to use Perry's expression, "passed out." Hot coffee and many blankets and at least three different remedies from the medicine chest presently left Joe out of pain, while in the case of Phil and "Brownie" the hot coffee and rest were alone sufficient.

Breakfast was rather late that morning, and Joe's place was vacant, for that youth was enjoying a sleep in the after cabin. "Brownie" and Phil, however, recovered wonderfully at the sight of bacon and eggs and did full justice to the repast. Steve laid down the law during breakfast as follows:

"After this there'll be no more swimming away from the boats, fellows. We came on this trip for fun and not funerals. You took a big chance, Phil, when you went that far out. This water's about ten degrees colder than what you and Joe are used to. It's a wonder you didn't both have cramps and drown."

"I guess it was rather foolish," agreed Phil. "The water was a lot colder out there than inside, too. Still it didn't bother me any." He lowered his voice, with a glance toward the companion way and the other cabin. "I thought old Joe was a goner, though, fellows. I was about forty feet away, I suppose, when I heard him yell, and before I could get back he'd gone down. I was afraid he meant to keep on going, but he thrashed his way up again and I managed to grab him. The trouble was then that he wanted to drown both of us and I had a hard time making him see reason."

"Someone ought to recommend you for the Carnegie Medal, Phil," said Han, with a laugh that didn't disguise his earnestness.

Phil shook his head. "I wasn't the hero of the adventure," he replied quietly. "I'm fairly at home in the water and I've done four miles without tiring much. It's 'Brownie' who deserves the medal, fellows. He saw Joe go down and jumped right in and beat it out there; and you all know that 'Brownie' isn't any swimmer. I think he was just about scared to death!"

"I'll bet he was," agreed Steve. "He's never been known to go ten yards from shore or boat. Yes, I guess 'Brownie' is the real hero, as you say, Phil."

"He certainly is, because I'll tell you frankly that I never could have got Joe in alone. I was just about used up by the time we'd tried to drown each other out there."

"We didn't know anything about it," explained Ossie, filling Phil's cup again unasked, "until someone happened to look from the *Follow Me* and saw you three out there. It was Tom Corwin, I think. I heard him yelling - I was getting my clothes on down here - and I ran up on deck and then grabbed the megaphone and shouted to Steve and Wink and the others who were over on the rock near the inlet. By the time they got it through their thick heads -"

"Thick heads be blowed!" exclaimed Steve disgustedly. "You were just yelling a lot of words that didn't mean anything. If you hadn't kept on pointing we'd never have known what was up. We all thought you had a fit."

All's well that ends well, however, and an hour after breakfast the incident was, if not forgotten, dismissed. Joe reappeared, looking rather pale still, but announcing himself quite all right. "I was nice and sick at my tummy," he explained, "and now I feel fine."

"Being sick at your tummy," remarked Perry unkindly, "is quite the best thing you do, Joe. If you can't be sea-sick you go and try to drown yourself!"

Of course "Brownie" was allowed to surmise that he had done something rather big, and Joe thanked him very nicely, but Mr. Carnegie is still in ignorance of his exploit!

The two boats floated out of the pool about ten and set off for Bar Harbor. The barely averted tragedy somewhat modified their regret at leaving Titania's Mirror and Mystery Island. Later, Steve and Joe tried to locate that island on the charts but without certain success. There were so many islands thereabouts that neither dared to more than guess at the identity of the one they had visited. Looking back at it from a distance of a half-mile they saw that it was in reality much smaller than they had supposed, being scarcely more than a huge rock pushed up from the ocean bed. Ossie, who had a leaning toward geology, furnished the theory that Mystery Island was no more nor less than the top of an extinct volcano and that Titania's Mirror was the crater.

"It probably sank, like lots of them did," he elaborated, "and the sea wore away part of it and flowed into the crater. I'm pretty sure that that rock we climbed out on this morning when we were swimming was volcanic."

"Sure," agreed Perry. "It was pumice stone. I meant to bring a bit of it along for you to clean your hands with."

"I didn't say pumice," replied Ossie haughtily. "It was more probably obsidian."

"My idea exactly! In fact, it had a very obstinate feeling. It - it left quite an impression on me!"

The *Follow Me* developed engine trouble that morning and they lay by for a half-hour or more while Tom Corwin toiled and perspired, argued and threatened. It was well after two o'clock when they ran up the eastern shore of Mount Desert Island and finally dropped anchor in Frenchman's Bay. They ate only a luncheon on board and then clothed themselves in their gladdest raiment and went ashore. They "did" the town that afternoon, mingling, as Wink said, with the "haut noblesse," and had dinner ashore at an expense that left a gaping hole in each purse. But they were both hungry and glad to taste shore food again, and no one begrudged the cost.

It was when they were on their way back to the landing that the glow of coloured lanterns behind a trim hedge drew their attention to the fact that someone was conducting a lawn party. The imposing entrance, through which carriages were coming and going, met their sight a moment later and inspired Perry with a brilliant idea.

"Say, fellows, let's go," he said, as they paused in a body to allow a handsome landau to enter. "I've never been to one of these lawn fêtes, or whatever they call them in the society papers, and here's the chance."

"Anybody invited you?" drawled Joe.

"No, but maybe they meant to. You can't tell. Maybe if they knew we were here -"

"Might send word in to them," suggested Wink Wheeler. "Say that the crews of the *Adventurer* and the *Follow Me* are without and -"

"Yes, without invitations," agreed Perry. "I get you, but that might cause our hostess embarrassment, eh? Why not just save her all that by dropping in sociably?"

"Are you crazy?" demanded Steve.

"Crazy to go and see all the pretty lanterns and things, yes. And maybe they'll have a feed, fellows! Come on! Take a chance! They can't any more than put us out! Besides, they probably won't know whether they invited us or not. It's just a lark. Be sports, fellows!"

The notion appealed to most of them, but Steve and Phil and Bert Alley declined to countenance it. "What will happen to you," said Steve grimly, "is that you'll all spend the rest of the night in the town jail for impersonating gentlemen!"

"Oh, if that's all you're afraid of," responded Perry sweetly, "you might as well come, too, Steve. They'd never charge *you* with that."

"Sub-tile, sub-tile," murmured Cas Temple.

"Anyhow, our clothes are perfectly O.K.," continued Perry. "White trousers and dark coats are quite *de rigor*. Come on, fellows."

They went on, all save the disapproving trio, Perry and Wink Wheeler leading the way up the winding avenue toward the glow of fairy lights ahead. No one challenged them, although they were observed with curiosity by several servants before they came out on a wide lawn in front of a spacious residence. Fully a hundred guests were already assembled. A platform overhung by twinkling and vari-coloured electric lamps had been laid for dancing and, as the uninvited guests paused to survey the scene, an orchestra, hidden by shrubbery and palms in tubs, started to play. Chairs dotted the lawn and a big marquee was nearby. On a low terrace in front of the hospitable doorway of the residence the hostess was receiving as the carriages rolled around the immaculate drive and stopped to discharge the guests. The boys viewed each other questioningly. Perry pulled down his waistcoat and walked boldly across the lawn and the drive and stepped to the terrace. Wink followed unhesitatingly, but the others hung back for a moment. Then they, too, approached, their assurance oozing fast. They reached the terrace in time to witness Perry's welcome.

"Good evening," said that youth in bored and careless tones, shaking hands with the middle-aged lady. "Awfully jolly night, isn't it!"

"How do you do, Mister - ah - so glad you could come. Yes, isn't it splendid to have such perfect weather? Marcia, you remember Mister - ah -"

Perry was passed on to a younger lady, evidently the daughter of the house.

"Howdy do?" murmured the latter, shaking hands listlessly.

"How do!" returned Perry brightly. "Bully night, eh!"

"Yes, isn't it?" drawled the young lady. Then Perry gave place to Wink.

"Good evening," said Wink, grinning blandly.

"Howdy do? So nice of you to come," murmured the lady. Wink joined Perry and they crossed to the other side of the terrace and maliciously watched the embarrassment of the other boys. Joe and Harry Corwin carried things off rather well, but the others were fairly speechless. Perry chuckled as he saw the growing bewilderment on the face of the hostess. But finally the ordeal was over and Perry led the way back to the festivities. Ossie groaned when they were safely out of ear-shot.

"She's on to us," he muttered. "I could see it in her eye! I'm off before they throw me out!"

"Don't be a jay," begged Perry. "The evening's young and the fun's just starting. Mrs. Thingamabob doesn't know whether she asked us or not. I'm going to see what's in the big tent over there. Come on, fellows."

They went, dodging their way between chattering groups and impeding chairs, but when Perry peered through the doorway of the marquee he was met with a chilly look from a waiter on guard there. "Supper is at ten o'clock, sir," said the servant haughtily.

"That's all right," replied Perry kindly. "Don't hurry on my account, old top!"

What to do for the succeeding hour was the question, for, while all save Perry and Ossie danced more or less skilfully, they knew no one to dance with. "If you ask me," remarked Cas Temple, yawning, "I call this dull. I'd rather be in my bunk, fellows."

"Well, let's find something to do," said Joe. "Maybe they've got a roller-coaster or a merry-go-round somewhere. Let's - um - explore."

By this time the dancing had begun in earnest and the platform was well filled with whirling couples. The boys paused to look on and, since the throng was growing larger every minute, were forced to change their position more than once with the result that presently Perry, Wink and Ossie found themselves separated from their companions. They looked about them unavailingly and waited for several minutes, and then, as the others did not appear, went on.

"We'll run across them," said Perry cheerfully. "Let's stroll around and see who's here."

"Awfully mixed crowd," said Wink. "Really, you know, Mrs. Jones-Smythe should be more particular. Why, some of the folks don't look as though they had ever been invited!"

"I know," agreed Perry, with a sigh. "Society's going to the dogs these days. One meets all sorts of people. It's perfectly deplorable."

"Beastly," agreed Ossie, stumbling over a chair. "Bar Harbor's getting very common, I fear."

RALPH HENRY BARBOUR

"Hello, that's pretty!" exclaimed Perry. They had emerged onto a walled space that looked straight out over the water. Hundreds of lights dotted the purple darkness and the air held the mingled fragrance of sea and roses. "This isn't so punk, you know," continued Perry, leaning over the wall. "Maybe this would suit me as well as an island."

"You're on an island," Ossie reminded him.

"I meant a real island," murmured Perry. Ossie was about to argue the matter when footsteps approached and they moved off again. A flight of steps led to a stone-floored verandah and they went up it and perched themselves on the parapet, to the probable detriment of the ivy growing across it, and watched the colourful scene. They were quite alone there, for the porch was detached from the terrace that crossed the front of the house. Two French windows were opened and beyond them lay a dimly-lighted library. Perry, hugging one foot in his hands, looked in approvingly.

"Whoever owns this shanty knows what's what," he said. "Just have a squint at all those books, will you? Millions of them! Wonder if anyone has ever read them."

"Well, I'm glad I don't have to," said Wink feelingly. "But that's a corking room, though. These folks must have slathers of money, fellows."

"Oh, fairly well fixed, I dare say," responded Perry carelessly. "Say, what time is it! Feed begins at ten, and with all that mob down there it's the early bird that's going to catch the macaroons. Wonder if they'll have lobster salad."

"Nothing but sandwiches and ices, I guess," said Ossie. "I wouldn't object to a steak and onions, myself. Funny how hungry you get up in this part of the world."

"You sure do," agreed Wink. "Let's move along. If the Corwin family gets in there ahead of us we might just as well pull in our belts and beat it."

"Let's go in through here," said Perry. "It's nearer, I guess." He started toward the first window.

"Oh, we'd better not," Ossie objected. "They might not like it."

"Piffle! They'll be tickled to death. They like folks to see their pretties." He stepped through the window and, dubiously, his companions followed. The library was a huge apartment, occupying, as it seemed to them, more than half the length of the house, with several long windows opening onto the terrace at the front. The furnishings were sombrely elegant and the dim lights caught the dull polished surface of mahogany and glinted on the gold-lettered backs of the shelf on shelf of books that hid the walls. Deep-toned rugs rendered footsteps soundless as they made their way toward the wide doorway at the far end of the room. They had traversed barely a third of the distance when a sudden sound brought them up short.

One of the windows that opened onto the terrace further along swung inward and a middle-aged man in evening attire stepped into the room. Perry, in spite of his former assurance, drew back into the shadow of a high-backed chair, stepping on Wink's foot and bringing a groan from that youth. The newcomer, however, evidently failed to hear Wink's protest, for, closing the window behind him in a stealthy manner, he crossed the further end of the library and paused beside a huge stone fireplace. Wink and Ossie had dropped to the protecting darkness of a big table, but Perry still peered, crouching, from behind the chair. In the dim light of an electric lamp the intruder's face had shown for an instant, and in that instant Perry had sensed it all! The stealthy manner of the man's entrance from the terrace instead of by the door, the plainly furtive way in which he crossed the room and the anxious expression of his face, a face which Perry saw at once to be criminal, was enough! The watcher was not in the least surprised when the man, hurriedly and still stealthily, drew out a square of mahogany paneling at the left of the fireplace and revealed the front of a small safe. Perry's heart began to thump agitatedly at the thought of witnessing a robbery. The man's fingers worked deftly at the knob. Perry could hear in the silence the click of the tumblers as they slid into place. Then the door was pulled open.

Between Perry and the robber lay a full thirty feet of floor, and a big table impeded his progress, but it took the boy less than a second to cover the distance, to seize the robber from behind, pinioning his arms, and to bear him heavily back to the floor.

CHAPTER XVII

FLIGHT

"Wink!" he cried. "Ossie! Come quick! Help here!"

The robber, having uttered a stifled cry of alarm at the instant of the unexpected attack, was now thrashing mightily about on the thick rug.

"Help!" he shouted. "Who are you? Let me go!"

"S-sh!" commanded Perry sternly, as the others plunged to his aid, overturning a chair on the way. "Be quiet! Sit on his legs, Ossie!" Perry was astride the man's chest, holding his arms to the floor. "Punch him if he makes a noise, Wink!" Perry, breathing hard, surveyed his captive in triumph. "Now then," he asked, "what have you got to say for yourself? What were you doing at that safe?"

The man glared in silence for an instant. To Wink it seemed that the emotion exhibited on the robber's countenance was amazement rather than fear.

"Come on," urged Perry. "What's the game?"

"Game!" choked the man, finding his voice at last. "Game? You - you young ruffians! You -"

"Cut that out, or I'll hand you something," growled Wink. "Answer politely."

"Let me up!"

"Nothing doing!" answered Perry. "Come across. What's your name and where do you come from? As you didn't get anything out of there, maybe we'll be easy with you if you talk quick."

"Let me suggest, if I may," said the man in a strangely quiet and restrained tone, "that you get off my stomach. This conversation can just as well be conducted under more comfortable conditions."

Perry blinked and Wink viewed the captive doubtfully.

"Promise not to try to run?" demanded Perry.

"I have no intention of running, thanks." The robber carefully dusted his clothes as he arose and then felt anxiously of a bruised elbow. "Now, if you will inform me what this - this murderous assault means I shall be greatly obliged to you."

"Suppose you tell us what you were doing at that safe?" said Perry sternly.

"Is that any of your business?" asked the other. It was evident that he was losing his temper again, and Wink drew a step nearer. "I presume I have a perfect right to open my own safe! What I wish to know -"

"Your own safe!" gasped Perry. "Oh, come now, you needn't try to tell us that you - you live here. You're a cracksman, my friend, that's what you are -"

Ossie tugged at Perry's sleeve, but Perry failed to notice it.

"One look at that face of yours is enough, old top," continued Perry. "It's got crook written all over it!"

"It has, has it?" gasped the man. "Let me tell you that my

name is Drummond, sir, and that this is my house, and that is my safe, and - and if you'll mind your own business -"

"What!" asked Perry weakly. "You mean that you - that this - you mean that -"

"I mean," interrupted the man angrily, "that I was about to deposit some money in that safe, some money I'd been carrying around in my pocket all the evening and feared I might lose, when you - you young thugs set on me and knocked me down! Knocked me down right in my own house, on my own hearth-rug! Why, you - you -"

Mr. Drummond's wrath got the better of his speech and he only sputtered, waving an accusing finger at the retreating Perry. Wink was already glancing about for a means of escape and Ossie was frankly deserting.

"I - I didn't know!" gasped Perry. "I - we saw you come in - and you looked like - like a -"

"You've said that already!" said the man, "Never mind my criminal looks, young man!"

"No, sir, we don't - I mean I was mistaken, sir! But, you see, it looked so - so queer, you coming in like that -"

"Queer! What was queer about it!" demanded Mr. Drummond irascibly, "No one but a parcel of young idiots would think it queer!" He took an envelope from his pocket, tossed it into the safe, closed door and panel and faced them again. "Who are you, anyway? I don't remember you."

"Er - my name - my name -" stammered Perry, "my name -"

"Well, well! Don't you know your name? Who invited you here?"

"Yes, sir, oh, yes, sir! It's Bush. We - you see, we were on the porch there, and we wanted to get back to the - the front of the house -"

"Who invited you here, tonight? Who -" The host's expression changed from indignation to suspicion. "Huh!" he ejaculated. "Robber, eh! Well, what were you doing in this room? Seems to me - hm! We'll look into this, I think!" He stepped back and touched a button in the wall. "We'll have this explained! We'll see who the robber is! We -"

"*Good night!*" Perry spurned the table against which he was leaning, hurdled a chair and plunged down the room. Ossie was at his heels and Wink was a good third. They fled at top speed and from behind them came the irate commands of their host:

"Stop! Come back! Stop, I say!"

But they didn't stop. They only ran faster. Wink beat Ossie to the first window easily and passed out even with Perry. And as they landed on the stone flagging outside they heard Mr. Drummond excitedly directing the pursuit.

"Quick, Wilkins! Get them! They tried to rob the house!" Mr. Drummond's voice pursued them along the verandah. "Help! Robbers! Head them off!"

The boys took the stone steps in two bounds, crashed at the bottom into a hedge, went tearing through and emerged beyond in a service yard, dimly lighted by one struggling electric bulb over a back doorway. It was Ossie who fell into the clothes basket and Wink who collided with the clothes reel and sent it spinning wildly and creakingly around in the darkness. Perry fortunately avoided all pitfalls and was leading by six yards when he reached the top of another flight of steps and saw the marquee and the dancing platform and the gay lights at his right. To make their way in that direction would be sheer folly, while in front of them lay a tangle of shrubbery and trees. Into this they hurtled, as from behind them came cries of "Stop, thief!" and the crunching of many footsteps.

Off went Wink's hat as he fled after the scurrying Perry. Ossie went down in a tangle of briars and prickly things with a grunt, rolled somehow clear and was off again. "This way!" shouted a voice. "I seen 'em! They went in here! Come on, men!"

Perry was running alongside a wall now, as he hoped, in the general direction of the street. Behind him came Wink and Ossie, crashing through shrubbery with a desperate disregard for noise. Then suddenly, the wall turned abruptly to the right. Perry stopped short, looked and decided.

"We've got to get over!" he gasped, as Wink ran blindly into him. "Give me a leg-up!"

Wink leaned weakly against the wall and Perry set a foot on his cupped hands and was just able to reach the top of the wall. But that was enough. Up he climbed. Then up came Ossie, and together, while the pursuit drew instantly closer, they pulled Wink to safety. For a brief moment they sat there and caught their breath while wondering what lay below them in the gloom of the further side. But there was scant time for conjectures, for the pursuit was in sight. Three bodies launched themselves into space, there was a frightful, devastating sound of breaking glass and the boys disengaged themselves from a cold-frame and sped on again into the darkness.

A house loomed suddenly before them, a house with lights and folks about the porch and a panting automobile curving its way down a drive. They turned to the right and kept along a lawn in the shadows of the trees. The automobile passed them with a purr and a sweeping flare of white light. Then Perry was after it and in another moment they were all three huddled somehow on the gas-tank at the rear and going with increasing speed out of the grounds and along a road. For a few minutes they hung there, breathing hard, and then Wink gasped:

"We've got to get off, Perry! It's going the wrong way!"

"If we do, we'll get killed," answered Perry. "Wait till it slows up."

They waited, but it seemed that it never would slow up. It went faster and faster. It passed houses and stores and a church. It went like the wind. Ossie groaned as they left the village behind.

"I can't stay on much longer, fellows!" he said hopelessly. "I'm clinging by my t-t-teeth!"

"You've got to!" answered Perry above the noise of the exhaust. "You'll break something if you don't! Wait till it slows up!"

Toot! Toot! To-o-oot! said the horn. And then, so suddenly that Perry's head collided with something particularly hard, the brakes squeaked harshly, the car slewed into an avenue and the boys, making the most of the opportunity, fell off. Ossie rolled a full half-dozen yards before his progress was stayed by a tree, and Wink, or so Perry declared afterwards, described a beautiful and quite perfect circle. Bruised, breathless and dizzy, they got to their feet and staggered to the side of the road and subsided on the turf.

After a long minute Ossie said feebly: "Where - do you - suppose - we are?"

"About ten miles - in the country," answered Wink.

There was silence then, silence long and profound. At last they climbed to their feet and, without speaking, walked off in the darkness in the direction from which they had come. Perhaps ten minutes later there came the first sound to break the silence. It was a choking sort of gurgle from Wink.

"What's the matter with you?" inquired Perry listlessly.

"I was just - just thinking," replied Wink. "It was so - so -" But words failed him and he began to laugh. After a dubious instant Perry chuckled, and then Ossie, and presently they were clinging to each other convulsively in the middle of the unknown road and sending shrieks of laughter up to the starlit sky.

Over an hour later they reached the landing. Both tenders were gone. The *Follow Me* was dark, but a faint light still burned aboard the *Adventurer*. Perry cupped his hands and sent a hail across the water. A sleepy response was followed by the sound of someone tumbling into the dingey and then by the measured creak of oars. Han was grumbling as he drew to the float.

"A fine time to be coming back," he said. "Where the dickens did you fellows get to, anyway? We looked all around the shop for you. Did you get any grub?"

"N-no," answered Perry, as he sank wearily into a seat. "We got tired of sticking around there and - and went for a ride."

"A ride? Where to?"

"Oh, just around a bit. Out in the country a ways. Was - was the grub any good?"

"Was it!" Han grew quite animated. "It was the best ever! They had about a dozen kinds of salad, and cold meats all over the place, and sandwiches and cakes and ice-cream and ices and coffee and -"

"Oh, shut up!" begged Ossie almost tearfully.

"It was bully! Were you there when we chased the burglars?"

"When you - what?" asked Wink.

"Chased the burglars, I said. Mr. Drummer, or something - I

never did get the name of the folks - found three of them trying to break into his safe, and they knocked him down and half-killed him, and the servants chased them, and then everyone took a hand! It was fine and exciting, I tell you! Had you gone off before that?"

"Why - er - seems to me we did hear something," said Perry. "When - when was this?"

"Oh, about a quarter to ten, I suppose. We were dancing -"

"*You* were dancing?" ejaculated Wink.

"Sure! All of us danced. Didn't you?"

"Who with, for the love of Mike?"

"Oh, lots of girls. Mrs. Thingamabob happened to find Joe standing around and made him tell her his name, and then she took him off and introduced him to some girls, and then he introduced the rest of us. It was a peachy floor. Some of the girls were all right, too."

"You seem to have got on fairly well," said Wink, "considering you weren't invited."

"We were invited just as much as you were," responded Han indignantly.

"Maybe, son, maybe," answered Wink, as he climbed aboard the darkened *Follow Me*, "but I'll bet they weren't half as sorry to see you go as they were to see us!"

With which cryptic remark Wink stumbled into the cockpit and disappeared.

CHAPTER XVIII

THE SQUALL

Although the Adventure Club remained in port for another day, neither Perry, Wink nor Ossie went ashore again, and all the efforts of the rest of the party failed to coax them off the boats. They were, they declared, fed up with Bar Harbor. And they hinted that so far as they were concerned the voyage might continue at any moment without protest. Han brought back a newspaper that afternoon containing a vivid and highly sensational account of the attempted robbery of the Alfred Henry Drummond "cottage." The three read it with much interest, and especially that portion of it which stated that "the local police force is investigating and has every expectation of making arrests within twenty-four hours, since it is not believed the burglars have succeeded in leaving the island and all avenues of escape are being closely guarded."

It might have been observed by the others, but wasn't, that Perry and Ossie, on the *Adventurer*, and Wink, on the *Follow Me*, exhibited a strange fondness for the seclusion of the cabins from that time until the next day at eight, when the cruisers up-anchored and passed out of the harbour. And as the broad Atlantic rolled under the keels three hearty sighs emerged from as many throats.

The two boats passed Petit Manan Island toward ten that forenoon, a tiny rocky islet holding aloft a tall shaft against the blue of the Summer sky. "A hundred and fourteen feet," said Joe informatively, " and the highest lighthouse on the coast except one."

RALPH HENRY BARBOUR

"Gee, think of living there in Winter!" said Perry awedly.

"Guess Petit Manan isn't as bad as some of the islands along here, at that," said Joe. "Some of them are a lot further from the mainland. Remember Matinicus?"

"Think of folks living on them," murmured Han. "They must be merry places in Winter with a blizzard blowing around! Lonely, wow!"

"Remember the white yacht we passed the other day near Burnt Coal?" asked Phil, looking up from the book he was reading. "The *Sunbeam* was the name of her. Well, a chap was telling me yesterday about her. It seems she's a sort of Mission boat, the Sea Coast Mission, I think it's called. The folks that live on these off-shore islands along here were in pretty bad shape a few years ago, bad shape in every way. There were no schools, or mighty few, and no churches, and the folks were just naturally pegging out from sheer loneliness and - and lack of ambition, just drifting right back into a kind of semi-civilized state, as folks do on islands in the Pacific that you read about. Well, someone realised it and got busy, and this Mission was started. There was a chap named MacDonald, Alexander MacDonald -"

"Sounds almost Scotch," observed Joe dryly.

"Never mind what he was. He's American now, if he was ever anything else," replied Phil warmly. "He was teaching school on one of the islands near Mount Desert in the Summers and going to college the rest of the time. There wasn't any church on this island and so he used to conduct services in the place they used for a school. Somehow, that put it into his head - or maybe his heart - to be a preacher. He preached around in all sorts of out-of-the-way places, and then this Mission started up and the folks behind it just naturally got hold of him and put him in charge. A New York woman had the *Sunbeam* built for him three or four years ago and now he lives right on it, he and a couple of men for crew, and she keeps pegging around the islands, up and down the coast, Summer and Winter. You fellows know what Doctor Grenfell does up around Labrador and beyond? Well, this Mr. MacDonald does the same stunt along this coast, and, by jiminy, fellows, it's some stunt! Think of plunging around these waters in Winter, eh? Breaking his own way through the ice often enough - the boat was built for it they say - and plugging through some of the nor'easters! Say, I take my hat off to that fellow!"

"Some job," agreed Steve thoughtfully. "Man's work, fellows."

"What does he do for 'em?" asked Ossie.

"Teaches them, son. Teaches them how to live clean, how to look after the kids, how to keep healthy. And prays with them, too, I guess. And brings them books and founds schools. Don't you guess that when this *Sunbeam* comes in sight of some of those little, forsaken islands the folks on shore sort of perk up? Guess the Reverend Mr. MacDonald is pretty always certain of a welcome, fellows!"

"Rather!" said Joe. "That's what I call - um - being useful in the world. Bet you he's a fine sort. Bound to be, eh?"

"I'd like to make a trip with him," said Perry. "Gee, but it would be some sport, wouldn't it? Talk about finding adventures! Bet you he has 'em by the hundreds."

"I dare say," said Phil, "that he'd be glad to dispense with a good many of them. Hope I haven't bored you, fellows," he added, returning to his book.

"You haven't, old scout," answered Han. "Any time you learn anything as interesting as that, you spring it. Blamed if it doesn't sort of make a fellow want to be of more use in the world. Guess I'll polish some brass!"

They passed many of those islands during the next few days, lonely, rock-girt spots scantily clad with wild grass and wind-worried fir trees. Sometimes there was a lighthouse, and nearly always the rocks were piled with lobster-traps, for lobstering is the chief industry of the inhabitants. They touched at one small islet one afternoon and went ashore. There were but three houses there, old, weather-faded shacks strewn around with broken lobster-pots and nets and discarded tin cans and rubbish. The folks they met, and they met them all, from babes in arms to a ninety-eight-year-old great-grandmother, looked sad and listless and run-to-seed. Even the children seemed too old for their years. It was all rather depressing, in spite of the evident kindliness of the people, and the boys were glad to get away again. They bought some lobsters and nearly a gallon of blueberries before they went. Ossie declared afterwards that those lobsters looked to him a sight happier than the folks they had seen ashore!

They went eastward leisurely, making many stops, and had fine weather until they sighted Grand Manan. Then a storm drove them to shelter one afternoon and they lay in a tiny harbour for two days while the wind lashed the ports and the rain drove down furiously. Nothing of great interest happened, although the time went fast and pleasantly. To be sure, there were minor incidents that Phil entered in the log-book he was keeping: as when Han fell overboard one morning in a heavy sea when the *Adventurer* was reeling off her twelve miles and was pretty well filled with brine and very near exhaustion when he reached the life-buoy they threw him. And once Ossie pretty nearly cut a finger off while opening a lobster. And then there was the time - it was during those two weather-bound days and everyone's temper was getting a bit short - when Perry cast aspersions on Ossie's biscuits at supper. Perry said they were so hard he guessed they were Ossie-fied, and the others laughed and Ossie got angry and they nearly came to blows: would have, perhaps, had not Steve promised to throw them both overboard if they did!

They spent two days at Grand Manan, and Perry, who had never before been further from Philadelphia than the Adiron-dacks, was vastly thrilled when he discovered that Grand

Manan was a part of New Brunswick. "This," he declaimed grandly as he stamped down on a clam-shell, "is the first time I've ever set foot on a foreign shore!"

The end of the first week in August found them harboured at Eastport. They stayed there four days, not so much because the place abounded in interest as because the *Adventurer*, who had behaved splendidly for several hundred miles, suddenly refused to go another fathom. Steve said he guessed the engine needed a good overhauling, and Perry chortled and offered his services to Joe to help take it apart. But Joe, in spite of his invaluable and ever-present hand-book, acknowledged his limitations, and the job went to a professional and the *Adventurer* spent most of three days tied up to a smelly little dock while the engine specialist took the motor down before be discovered that a fragment of waste and other foreign matter had lodged in the gasoline supply pipe. Fortunately, his charge was moderate. Had it been otherwise they might have had to stay in Eastport until financial succour reached them, for the exchequer was almost depleted.

They found a letter from Neil among the mail that was awaiting them at Eastport. Neil was evidently down on his luck and begged for news of the club. He got it in the shape of an eight-page epistle from Phil.

Perry made a close study of the sardine industry and laid gorgeous plans for conducting a similar venture on the banks of the Delaware when he returned home. "You see," he explained, "a sardine is just whatever you like to call it in this country. I used to think that a sardine had to come from Sardinia."

"From where?" asked Ossie, the recipient of Perry's confidences.

"Sardinia."

"Where's that?"

"I dunno. Spain, I think. Or maybe Italy. Somewhere over there." He waved a hand carelessly in the general direction of Grand Manan. "Anyway, there's nothing to it. A man told me this morning that the sardines they use here are baby herring or menhaden or - or something else. I guess most any fish is a sardine here if it's young enough. Unless it's a whale. Now why couldn't you use minnows? There are heaps of minnows in the Delaware River. Or young shad. A shad's awfully decent eating when he's grown up, and so it stands to reason that he'd make a perfectly elegant sardine."

"Nothing but bones," objected Ossie.

"A young shad, say a week-old one, wouldn't have any bones, you chump. At least, they'd be nice and soft. It's a dandy business, Ossie. All you have to have is some fish and a lot of oil and some tin cans."

"Sounds easy the way you tell it. I suppose you pour the oil in the tin can and drown the fish in the oil and clamp the lid on, eh?"

"N-no, there's a little more to it than that. There's something about boiling them. They have big kettles. Want to go over this afternoon and see them do it? There's a fine, healthy smell around there!"

"Thanks, but I got a whiff of it a while ago. Unless you want me to sour on sardines, Perry, you won't take me to the place they build them."

The engine was reassembled in the course of time and, with fresh supplies, the *Adventurer* turned homeward, the *Follow Me* close astern. They started after an early dinner, having decided to make Northeast Harbor that evening and proceed to Camden the next day. They had seen enough of the eastern end of the coast, they thought, while from Camden westward there were numerous places that had looked enticing. So "No Stop" was the order, and the *Adventurer*, turning back into home waters off Lubec, churned her way through the Bay of Fundy at a good pace. The morning had dawned hazy, but the sun had shone brightly for awhile in mid-afternoon. Later the sunlight disappeared again and the northern sky piled itself with clouds. South West Head was abeam then and Steve half-heartedly offered to run to shelter. But the others pooh-poohed the suggestion.

"If we duck every time there's a cloud," said Joe, "we'll never get back to Camden. There isn't any wind and the barometer says fair."

The barometer was rather a joke aboard the *Adventurer*. It hung just inside the forward companion way and was undoubtedly a most excellent instrument. But not a soul aboard could read it properly. When it dropped, the skies cleared and the wind blew. When it rose, it invariably rained or got foggy. Steve had long since given it up in despair, but Joe still maintained a belief in his powers of prognosticating weather by the barometer, a belief that no one else on the boat shared.

"If the pesky thing says that," remarked Han, "it'll snow before night! Still, I don't see why we need to run into harbour yet. There's no sign of fog, and if it's only rain that's coming, why, we've been wet before. I say let her flicker, Steve."

"I guess so. We're not out far and if it does get very wet we can soon get under cover somewhere. Find me the next chart, Joe, will you?"

They could see the Seal Islands, or they thought they could, off to port at a little past three. The *Follow Me* was hiking along about a quarter of a mile astern, making better going than the *Adventurer*, just as she always did in a heavy sea. And today the sea was piling up a good deal. Joe looked anxious at times, but he had passed his novitiate and now it took a good deal of tossing to send him below. What happened at about half-past three occurred so suddenly that no one aboard the *Adventurer* was prepared for it.

It grew dark almost between one plunge of the cruiser's bow and another, and before Steve could punch out his warning on the whistle, preparatory to heading to starboard, a gust of wind tore down on them from the north like a blast from the pole and set canvas rattling and flags snapping. Steve headed toward Englishman's Bay, nine miles due west, and the *Follow Me* altered her course accordingly. But that storm had no intention of awaiting anyone's pleasure. The first gust was quickly followed by a second and the sky darkened rapidly. The spray began to come over the rail, and Han and Perry tugged down a flapping curtain and lashed it to the stanchions. The next time Steve looked for the *Follow Me* she was no longer in sight, for the darkness had closed in between the two craft.

"This is a mess," shouted Steve, peering through the spray-wet glass ahead. "I wish we were about seven or eight miles further along, fellows."

"Well, we will be presently," replied Phil cheerfully. "I dare say this blow won't last long. It's only a squall, probably."

"It's a good one, then," muttered Steve. "If you don't believe it take hold of this wheel. Feel her kick? Keep a lookout for that island in there, Joe."

Things went from bad to worse and ten minutes after the first warning the *Adventurer* was tossing about like a cork, her propeller as often out of water as in, and making hard work of it.

They had to hold tight to whatever was nearest to keep from being pitched across the bridge deck. The seas began to pile in over the roof of the after cabin and the deck was soon awash. Steve held to the wheel like grim death, with Joe at his side when needed, and they plunged on. But it didn't take Steve long to realise that to attempt to make the haven under such conditions would be folly. There were islands and reefs ahead and the gloom made it impossible to see for any distance.

"The only thing we can do, fellows," he said presently, shouting to make himself heard above the wind, "is to run for it straight down the shore. If we can get in past Wass Island we can anchor, I guess, but if we try to make Englishman's Bay we'll pile up somewhere as sure as shooting! I wish I was certain the *Follow Me* was all right."

"If we are, she's sure to be," said Joe. "She's a nifty little chip in tough weather. Here comes some rain, Steve!"

Joe's description was weak, however. It was more than "some" rain; it was a deluge! It swept past the edges of the curtains and splashed on the deck in dipperfulls. And it hid everything beyond the torn and tattered Union Jack at the bow. Looking through the dripping windows was like looking through the glass side of an aquarium, for beyond it was a solid sheet of water. Steve gazed anxiously from chart to compass under the electric lights and eased off to port.

"There's too much land around here," he shouted to Joe, "to leave me happy. And, what's more, I'm none too certain just where we are at this blessed minute. So it's the wide ocean for yours truly. We'll just have to run for it and trust to luck!"

"Right-o," called Joe sturdily. "Let her flicker, old man! There's one thing plumb certain, and that is if we come across an island we're - um - likely to run clean over it!"

But Joe was wrong.

The words were scarcely off his lips when a cry of mingled astonishment and alarm sprang from Steve as he threw his weight on the wheel. At the same moment there was a shock that sent all hands reeling, the *Adventurer* quivered from stern to stern, and then, after a moment no longer than a heart-beat, lurched forward again. Directly over the bow, glimpsed vaguely through the rain and gloom, rose a towering cliff. Steve's frantic efforts were in vain, for although he tore at the clutch and the propeller thrashed the water astern, the *Adventurer* was already in the smother of the surf and an instant later she struck.

CHAPTER XIX

SHIPWRECKED

Afterwards the boys looked back on the ensuing five minutes as a dream rather than a reality. The cruiser grounded with an impetus that set pans rattling in galley, lifted again and once more thumped her stern down, as she did so swinging her stern slowly around in a last frantic effort to pull clear. Then the boat careened, a sea washed clean across the deck and, with her keel forward of the engine firmly imbedded in the sand, she lay still save for the tremors that shook her when the angry surf rushed in across her beam.

There was confusion enough, but on the whole the six alarmed boys behaved sensibly. Steve, wet to his waist, turned off the engine and banged shut the chart-box even as he shouted his orders. "Life preservers, fellows! Han, get the big cable from the locker. Keep your heads now!"

Clinging like a leech to the canted roof of the forward cabin, Steve himself worked along with the rope and, half-drowned in rain and surf, made it fast to the cleat. The others, struggling into life-belts, clung to the stanchions or whatever they could find. Steve crawled back with the coil, drenched and breathless.

"We've got to get off, fellows," he said. "It's only a dozen yards to the beach and we can make it all right. Close every hatch. Ossie, fetch a can of biscuits. See that the lid's tight." Wave after wave struck on the starboard beam and fell hissing across the boat. The side curtains were ripped from the stanchions

RALPH HENRY BARBOUR

and fluttered wildly about them.

"Going to swim for it?" asked Joe above the roar of waves and tempest.

"Yes! We've got to. The boat would swamp in an instant. I'll start ahead with the line. You fellows wait and then follow it in."

"Better let me go along," said Joe, his hands formed into a speaking-trumpet.

"No need. I'll make it."

"Look out for back-tow!"

The other nodded. He had pulled off his coat and unlaced his shoes and now he dropped these things through the forward hatch and wrapped the big rope around his waist. "Better not try to swim with your coats, fellows," he instructed. "Nor shoes. Don't take any chances. Last man off see that this hatch is shut tight." He crawled around the stanchions on the starboard side and crept along to the bow, the others, huddled together on the sloping bridge, watching anxiously. Then he slipped from sight. Once they saw his head, or thought they saw it, a darker blot in the grey-green welter. Joe was already creeping toward the bow, and, having reached it, he crouched there, blinded by rain and spray, and waited for the rope to tauten. It seemed a long while before he waved an arm to the watchers behind and swung himself off. They saw his hands travel along the rope a moment and then he was smothered up in the spume.

One by one the others followed without misadventure save when Han slipped on the deck and would have rolled across and plunged over the further side had he not fortunately caught the iron support of the searchlight in front of the funnel. Phil was the last to go. With a final look about the deck as he clung to an awning pipe, he followed Ossie. The latter was swinging himself hand-over-hand by the rope with the waves surging to his shoulders. Then Phil saw him strike out and the waters hid him. The beach was visible at moments from the bow, and once Phil, as he prepared to swing himself off, thought he saw figures there. Then he, too, was battling. The waves swept him under the rope and would have wrenched him from it had he not clung on desperately. Holding to it with his right hand, he sought to find it with his left and so draw himself on, but the surf swirled him about dizzily and he gave up the attempt. Instead, almost drowned in the smother, he used his left arm and his legs for swimming, edging his right hand along the cable as best he could, and presently, although none too soon, felt the churning gravel beneath his stockinged feet. But when he tried to stand, the receding water swept his legs from under him so unexpectedly and forcibly that he lost his grasp of the rope. He went down and felt the water tugging him back, swam mightily and was lifted to the top of an in-rushing breaker, filled his lungs with air and felt blindly for the rope. Then hands seized him and Joe and Han, clinging to the cable, dragged him ashore.

Phil found himself under the frowning battlement of the huge cliff on a ledge of sand and shingle scarcely twenty feet wide. But there was less sweep for the rain here and the *Adventurer* was plainly visible through the strange semi-darkness. Steve had made the shore end of the cable fast to a boulder that stood, half out of the shingle, at the base of the cliff. For a long minute the six boys huddled there in the storm and disconsolately gazed at the boat. It was Han who voiced the thought of most of them.

"She won't stay together long, I guess," he said sorrowfully. "Those waves will batter her to pieces."

"She'll stand a lot of battering," answered Steve hopefully. "It's hitting her on the beam and she hasn't swung much since I left her. The tide's still coming in and -" He stopped. Then: "I ought to have dropped the stern anchor over," he went on.

"What an idiot! If she had that to hold her from swinging broadside -"

"Would it hold her?" asked Joe dubiously.

"It would help." Steve tightened his belt. "I'm going back," he said.

They remonstrated, but to no purpose. Then Joe and Han wanted to go along, and were denied. "It's no trick," said Steve resolutely. "I can do it easily. You fellows stand by when I come ashore again. That's the only tough part of it. Someone might see if there's a way up from this beach. If the tide comes much higher it's going to be a bit damp here."

It was Perry who undertook that task, while the others followed Steve to the breakers' edge and watched him return to the *Adventurer*. He made no attempt to swim, but pulled himself along by the line, hand-over-hand, his head for the most of the time under the water. But presently he emerged and they saw him clamber to the deck, crawl along it and disappear. He seemed a long time there, but he came into sight again eventually and began the return trip. Perry was back by then and they formed a line by clasping hands and Joe stood well above his waist, battered by the surf, and Steve was helped along from one to another and presently they were all back on the beach once more.

"I got it over," gasped Steve, "but it was hard work. I think it will hold. If the storm will only go down pretty soon she may get through. I think some of her planks are sprung, though. There's a foot of water in the after cabin. I got some matches and this cup." He pulled a tin cup from a trousers pocket. "Can we get up the cliff a way?"

"Yes," answered Perry. "There's a sort of a shelf about a hundred feet beyond there. I'll show you the way."

They followed. Real darkness was coming fast now and Perry

found difficulty in retracing his steps. But in a few minutes, by dint of scrambling and pulling themselves upward, they reached the shelf. It was barely large enough to hold them all and was scarcely ten feet above the level of the beach below. Nor was it at all level, for it had been formed by the accumulation of falling debris from the cliff and sloped outward at a steep angle. Some dwarf firs and low bushes had gained rootage, however, and it was possible for them to huddle there without fear of rolling to the rocks beneath. Steve tried to find some dead branches to build a fire, and did succeed in getting a few, but his first attempt to set them alight proved the futility of the undertaking. There was nothing for it save to lie as close together as they could, for warmth, and await the morning.

That was a miserable night. They all slept at times, and by changing places they all, for a while at least, found some degree of warmth. But they had been drenched through to start with and when, at last, the stormy world began to lighten their garments were still sodden and they shivered whenever they stirred. Ossie was ill toward morning, but there was nothing they could do for him except huddle closely about him. He complained of intense pains in his chest and Steve had horrible visions of pneumonia until Ossie, asked to locate the trouble more definitely, laid a trembling hand on a portion of his anatomy and muttered "Here" through chattering teeth.

"That's not your chest, you idiot," said Steve, vastly relieved. "That's your stomach!"

"Is it?" returned the sufferer miserably. "Well, it hurts just the same!"

But after an hour he felt considerably better and went off to sleep. By that time it was early morning and they could see about them. The rain had almost ceased, but the wind still blew hard and the surf was still pounding. Once during the darkness the waves had, from the sound, entirely covered the little beach. Now, however, they had receded and, as the light grew, they saw that the *Adventurer* lay, with regard to the tide, about as they had last glimpsed her. But she had swung her stern further around, in spite of the anchor Steve had dropped, and the waves were breaking almost squarely across her. She was a pathetic sight. Her side curtains were waving in ribands, the forward flag-pole held nothing but one tiny rag of blue bunting and the tender, torn from the chocks, was jammed between the stanchions ahead.

"But she's still whole," said Steve from between blue lips. "And the storm's going down. If she isn't sprung too much, and we could only get her off of there -"

"Getting her off," said Joe with a pessimism born of hunger and cold and the gloom of the early morning, "will be about as easy as moving a house with a toothpick. I dare say the sand's bedded around her two feet high."

"I'm afraid so," Steve agreed. "Well, let's have something to eat. Will you have steak or chicken, Joe?"

"Broiled ham and a baked potato, please, and a couple of eggs. Not more than two minutes for the eggs. And you might bring me a couple of hot biscuits -"

"Oh, shut up," begged Steve miserably.

"Well, you started it! Who's awake here?"

"I am," muttered Perry. "Seems to me I haven't been anything but awake for ten years."

"Well, want to order your breakfast now, or will you wait?" asked Joe cheerfully.

"Guess I'll wait," answered Perry grimly. "Where are those crackers?"

They got Ossie awake with difficulty and Steve doled out six crackers to each. The tin cup came in handy, for there was a pool of rain water in a ledge below them.

"What I can't see," grumbled Ossie, "is why we didn't stay on board the boat. It would have been a lot drier than this place."

"You may think so now," replied Steve, "but wait till you get aboard again. We might have stayed on her, as it's turned out, but the boat didn't look very homelike to me yesterday!"

"How the dickens were we to know that it would hold together, or even stay on its keel?" asked Joe disgustedly. "Don't talk like a sick goldfish, Ossie!"

As soon as they had consumed breakfast they scrambled down to the beach with many groans and stretched their cramped and aching limbs. The rain, although now little more than a very heavy mist, limited their vision to a hundred yards or so in any direction. Steve hazarded the opinion that they were not more than two miles from the mainland, although he made no attempt to give a name to the island they were on. The fate of the *Follow Me* worried them all, but Phil, always the most sanguine in times of stress, pointed out that as the other craft had not followed them onto the island she was probably safe.

"She may be piled up further along somewhere," suggested Joe. "I say we'd better have a look. It would help a bit to know what sort of a place we've struck, anyway. For all we know there may be a house just around the corner!"

So they set out in two parties, Steve, Ossie and Phil going one way and the rest the other. It was agreed that they were to be back in an hour at the most. Twenty minutes later, each exploration party having stuck to the beach, they came together again, much to their mutual surprise.

"The pesky thing isn't more than a few acres big!" exclaimed Joe disgustedly.

"And it's entirely surrounded by water," added Perry brightly.

"Most islands are," said Ossie. "We can get up on top easily enough here, fellows. Let's see what it looks like."

Their island was little more than a rock stuck out of the water. Just how big it was was difficult to determine since the haze of driving mist allowed but little view. From the beach, at a point presumably directly opposite the place where they had come ashore they climbed by the aid of rocky footholds and bushes to a broken but generally level summit clad with a tangled growth of blueberry and briars and sprinkled most liberally with boulders. The ground arose gradually as they advanced, guided by Steve's pocket compass, and before very long they reached the wind-swept edge of the cliff against which they had spent the night. From the summit they could see dimly at brief intervals the form of the *Adventurer* far below.

"Well, I don't see that we've accomplished much," said Han. "We're here, but where are we? And how the dickens are we going to get back again? If anyone thinks that I'm going to risk my neck sliding down here he's mistaken."

"We don't ask you to, Ossie dear," said Han. "Your little neck is much too precious. One thing is certain, anyway, I guess: there's no hotel on the place!"

"Hotel!" said Joe. "Gee, I'd be satisfied with a - um - cow-shed!"

Nevertheless, they made the return journey in better spirits, for they had walked the aches from their limbs and warmth into their bodies. On the way Steve made them gather fagots of dead branches and they found a number of larger pieces of wood on the beach. By the time they were once more "at home," as Perry put it, they had all the material for a fire save paper or some other form of kindling. Steve experimented with twigs from the fir trees on the ledge, but they were too wet to burn. No one had any paper, or if they had it was too damp.

"What would Robinson Crusoe have done?" asked Steve, frowning thoughtfully.

Joe, who had seated himself tiredly on the wet sand and was digging his stockinged heels into it, sneered at Mr. Crusoe. "He'd have made a trip on his raft," he said, "and fetched ashore a bundle of kindling. If it hadn't been for that wreck to draw on Robinson Crusoe would have starved to death in twenty-four hours!"

"Of course!" exclaimed Steve. "That's the idea!"

"What, starve?" asked Joe distastefully.

"No, you idiot, go out to the *Adventurer* and get some gasoline!"

"Sure!" agreed Ossie. "Only - just when we were getting dry at last -"

"What's the matter with stripping," asked Steve cheerfully, suiting action to word. "Is there a can or anything I can put it in, Ossie?"

"There's a jug in the starboard locker. There's about a pint of vinegar in it, but I guess we can sacrifice that."

"Drink it, Steve, and save it," suggested Perry.

The tide had retreated further by now and the bow of the cruiser was almost beyond the breakers and Steve's journey was not difficult. When he got back, with the vinegar jug filled with gasoline hung around his neck, he reported the *Adventurer* waist-deep in water at the stern. "You fellows start the fire," he said, "and I'll go back and bring some grub ashore. There's no reason for starving with food handy."

Joe volunteered to accompany him, and, after disrobing and putting his damp clothes under a stone to keep them from blowing away, he and Steve plunged back into the water. Meanwhile success met the efforts of the firemen and soon a good-sized blaze was roaring in spite of wind and mist. They had located it as near the foot of the cliff as possible and, although the smoke made itself disagreeable by billowing out in their faces, it was thereby somewhat sheltered from the elements. Steve and Joe made three trips and brought back frying-pan, coffee-pot and smaller utensils, as well as provisions, and a half-hour later they were beginning a supplementary breakfast of bacon and coffee. And if anything in all the wide world, from the time of Noah to that of the Adventure Club, ever tasted sublime to a shipwrecked mariner it was that same bacon and coffee!

When they had finished, Phil's watch - the only one of six which had neither run down for lack of winding or been incapacitated by immersion in salt water - gave the hour as twenty minutes past seven. Comforted by food and drink, they warmed themselves at the fire and waited for the tide to recede far enough to allow a survey of the *Adventurer*. The comfort was too much for Perry and he fell asleep with his feet almost in the embers and his head on a rock and slumbered emphatically. At last the line of breakers was well astern of the cruiser and the boys, leaving their stockings to dry by the fire and rolling their trousers up, began their investigation.

On the whole the *Adventurer* had so far come off easily. Her planks had been strained in several places, but there were no breaks. Steve, hanging over the stern, tried to get sight of the propeller but failed, as the sand had settled about it. Joe, wading out into the water, had better success when he investigated. He came up, dripping, with the welcome announcement that the blades were intact and that, so far as he could ascertain by feeling, the shaft was not bent. But things looked pretty dismal below-decks. The forward cabin was awash, as was the engine-well, and the after stateroom was knee-deep. They gathered on the bridge deck and held council.

"We can plug her seams, all right," said Steve, "and by keeping a pump going get to port, *if* we can only get her off the beach. But I can't, for the life of me, see how we're going to do that. Her bow's settled a foot deep in sand and it's piled up along this side of her. Even her propeller's buried!"

"Not very much," said Joe. "If we start her she'll kick it away in a minute."

"But there isn't any use starting her," said Steve thoughtfully, "unless she's afloat a good deal more than she was this morning. If only we had something to fix a line to astern we might pull her off with the windlass." His gaze ran seaward and in an instant he was on his feet gazing intently through the mist. "What's that back there?" he demanded eagerly. "Isn't it a rock, fellows?"

CHAPTER XX

THE DERELICT

It was a rock whose brown head was thrust barely two feet above the water.

"It's the ledge we grazed last night," cried Joe. "Could we get a rope to that, Steve?"

"Why not? We'll have a go at it, anyway. Help me with the tender, someone!"

It was difficult work. As a first step the bow line was replaced by a smaller rope and taken through the breakers to the out-cropping ledge. There, working precariously in the water while Joe held him from the boat and Han did his best to keep the dingey steady, Steve eventually got the big cable around the rock, protecting it from the rough edges by a blanket from one of the berths. Fortunately, the rock was so formed that, once drawn tight, there was no danger of the rope slipping off, and they returned to the *Adventurer*, Steve towing behind, in triumph. In the meanwhile the others, directed by Phil, were stuffing the worst of the seams with strips of muslin, using table knives for caulking irons. The cable to the rock was led through a ring at the stern and carried forward to the windlass. By the time the tide had begun to rise again they had got the hull free of water, taking turns at the hand-pump and operating the bilge-pump at the same time. Then they waited to see how well they had succeeded at their caulking. It was noon by that time, and they ate cold rations in the galley, and while they were below a transient gleam of sunlight shone for an instant through the hatch above and they tumbled to deck. The fine rain had almost ceased and although the sunlight was gone again, the clouds were breaking. Steve whooped for joy and the others joined him. It might have been only in imagination, but it seemed that the wind was less fierce and that the in-rolling breakers were less formidable.

There was little to do save to set the cruiser as much to rights inside and out as was possible and wait for high tide again. As the water once more surrounded the boat they were pleased and encouraged to find that while the water was again coming in through the seams it filled the bilge so slowly that the pump could easily take care of it. Perry declared proudly that they had done a "caulking job!" They went ashore before the water cut them off entirely and built the fire up again. About four the wind died down appreciably and the sun, which had been flirting with the world ever since noon, burst forth in a sudden blaze of glory. The mist disappeared as if by magic and exclamations of surprise burst from six throats as eager eyes looked shoreward.

There, as it seemed scarcely a half-mile distant, was the mainland; green fields, grey cliffs, white houses! In reality the distance was well over a mile and a quarter, but so clear had the atmosphere suddenly become that the space of tumbled green water intervening looked hardly more than a swimmer's stunt! They cheered and would have waved their caps had they had any to wave. A small steamer was ducking her way along near shore and they could almost see the spray tossing from the bow. They found a nearer way to the top of the cliff and climbed to the summit and tried to decide just where they were, but even Steve was at a loss, although he was fairly certain that Englishman's Bay was well to the north, probably as far distant as six miles. But, since from where they gazed islands and mainland melted into each other, even Wass Island was not determinate. But after all it didn't much matter where they were. In a calm sea they could reach the shore in the dingey if it became necessary, while a distress signal would undoubtedly be soon seen from the nearer head-land. But

RALPH HENRY BARBOUR

Steve was not ready to call for aid yet, and together they made their way back to the beach and settled down philosophically to await evening and high tide.

With the prospect of release from their desert island to cheer them, waiting was not so hard. They had some supper about six and after that the time passed fairly quickly. At half-past eight they made their way out to the *Adventurer*. The wind had died entirely down at sunset and now the sea was probably as quiet and well-behaved as it ever was just there. About nine they began operations. No one was too sanguine of the results, but when, having started the engine and experimentally moved the clutch into reverse to clear the sand from around the propeller, no untoward incident happened they became more encouraged. The heaving lever was put into the windlass and, with Phil astern to watch the cable where it ran through the ring bolt, Steve operated the engine while the others took turns, two and two, at the windlass. Gradually the manila cable tightened and strained and the screw churned hard, but the *Adventurer*, save for righting herself a trifle, gave no indication of moving from her sandy bed. Steve summoned the boys who were not working the windlass to the after part of the boat in order to lighten the bow as much as possible, and they worked on. Just when it seemed that not another inch of the cable was to be conquered there was a shout from Ossie and Han, who were panting at the lever, and the *Adventurer* moved!

After that it was only a matter of time. Inch by inch the cruiser dragged her keel along the sand, each minute floating a little freer and each minute putting her deck more level as the stern found the deep water. And, perhaps a half-hour from the time they had started, they had the boat riding clear and slowly going astern to take up the cable. It was out of the question to get the rope free of the rock and so they had to cut it, and, having done so, they swung cautiously around in a wide circle and headed toward the cheerful white beam of a lighthouse that beckoned from the shore.

They had to keep the pump going, for a leak they had not

suspected developed forward, but that was a small matter and they were so glad to get out of the adventure with nothing worse than a few sprung planks, some bent stanchions and the loss of the side curtains that they would willingly have pumped by hand. Half an hour later, after a slow and careful passage from island to mainland, with the searchlight picking out her path, the *Adventurer* dropped anchor in a narrow harbour.

They stayed there only overnight, for in the morning they found that there was no prospect of getting repairs made there, and so, with the bilge pump sucking merrily, they ran ten miles further down the coast and before dinner time saw the *Adventurer* on a cradle and hauled high and dry from the water. The damage to the hull, while nowhere severe, was more general than they had thought, and the man who was to do the repairs decreed a week's stay. After discussing the situation it was decided that all save Steve and Phil were to proceed to Camden by rail and wait there for the *Adventurer*. Steve was to remain to superintend the repairs and painting - the cruiser stood in need of paint by then - and Phil volunteered to keep him company and help take the boat on when it was ready.

In the meanwhile, after a day of uncertainty, the *Follow Me* was located by telegraph at Jonesport. "All well. Sailing for Camden tomorrow. Meet you there" was the reply from Harry Corwin. Steve and Phil, watching seaward from the deck of the *Adventurer*, sitting high up on a marine railway, thought that they made out the *Follow Me* about ten o'clock the next morning, but couldn't be sure. The two boys, captain and first mate, lived aboard and took their meals wherever they could get them. They were there just six days and had a very happy if unexciting time. Several absurd epistles reached them from Camden, all of which indicated that the other members of the Adventure Club were enjoying themselves hugely. At last, shining with new paint and polished brass and refurnished with new curtains, the *Adventurer* slid down the railway again, floated out from the cradle and pointed her nose toward Penobscot Bay. In the middle of a bright Friday afternoon she dropped anchor alongside her companion craft, Phil doing wild and ecstatic things with the whistle and eliciting no response from the *Follow Me*. Steve and Phil donned proper shore-going togs and tumbled into the dingey. The *Follow Me* was totally deserted, which accounted for the fact that, while their noisy arrival had aroused not a little interest on other craft, the *Follow Me* had received them very coldly. They found some of the party at the hotel and the others rounded up later. Everyone was flatteringly glad to see the new arrivals again, but none more so than Perry. Perry was absolutely pathetic in his greetings and refused to let Steve out of his sight for an instant.

"I'm quite taken by surprise," declared Steve. "I knew you loved me devotedly, Perry, but this is - this is really touching!"

Perry grew a trifle red and coughed. "Er - well - I hope so," he blurted.

"You hope so? Hope what?"

"Hope it's touching," explained the other, grinning. "You see, I'm flat broke, Steve, and so is everyone else, or pretty near, and if you could lend me a couple of dollars -"

"I feared it wasn't all just affection," sighed Steve, reaching for his purse. "But it was worth the price, Perry!"

"Much obliged! You - you might make it three, if you don't mind. I owe Han fifty cents and Ossie a quarter - no, thirty-five -"

"Here's five, you spendthrift. Let me have it back as soon as you can, though, for I'm down near the bottom myself."

"I will, Steve. I've sent for some and it ought to be along in a day or two. Money doesn't last any time here!"

Friends and acquaintances made during their former visit had done everything possible to make the boys' stay so very more than pleasant, and when the matter of going on was introduced the suggestion met with scant sympathy. However, Steve was not at all averse to a week or so of lotus eating and, having satisfied his conscience by the proposal, he settled down, to enjoy himself with the rest. His friends ashore were lavish with hospitality, while "Globbins the Speed Fiend," as Perry had dubbed the freckle-faced proprietor of the restless automobile, was indefatigably attentive. A second letter from Neil, forwarded from one port of call to another in their wake, reached them one day, and they composed a reply between them and all hands signed it. Neil was having rather a dull time of it, they gathered, and they hoped their letter would cheer him up a bit.

At last, when they had, after two postponements, fixed a day of departure, a storm that tied up shipping all along the North Atlantic Coast for four days caused a final delay, and consequently it was well toward the last of August when they said good-bye and set forth for Squirrel Island. No one particularly cared to visit Squirrel Island save Han, who had friends there, but as there was still a full week at their disposal they were in no great hurry and one port was as good as another. They remained there a day and then made Portland. At Portland supplies were put in, and one Wednesday morning they picked up the anchor at a little after six o'clock and started for Provincetown with the fine determination to cover the distance of approximately a hundred and twenty-five miles before they sat down to supper. That they didn't do so was no fault of either the *Adventurer* or the *Follow Me*.

It was about half-past eight that Phil, sitting on the forward cabin roof with his back braced against the smokestack, called Steve's attention to an object far off to port. They had then put some thirty miles between them and Portland and were twenty miles off Cape Neddick. The morning was lowery, with occasional spatters of rain, and the storm, which had blown off to the northward the day before, had left a heavy sea running. For an hour the *Adventurer* and the *Follow Me* had been climbing up the slopes of grey-green swells and sliding down into swirling troughs, and for a minute Steve couldn't find the dark speck at which Phil was pointing. When he did at last sight it over the tumbled mounds of water he stared in puzzlement a moment before he took the binoculars from their place and fitted them to his eyes. He looked long and then silently handed the glasses through the window to Phil, punched two shrill blasts on the whistle and swung the wheel to port.

"Looks like a wreck," said Phil, after an inspection of the distant object. "Going to see?"

Steve nodded. "Might be someone aboard," he answered. "We can tell in another mile or so, I guess."

Phil gave up the glasses to the others, who had clustered to the bridge, while the *Follow Me* altered her course in obedience to the signal, her company probably wondering why Steve had suddenly chosen to stand out to sea. At the end of ten minutes it was plainly to be determined with the aid of the binoculars that the object which had attracted their attention and curiosity was without any doubt a wreck, and as the *Adventurer* drew momentarily closer her plight was seen to be extreme. Whether anyone remained aboard was still a question when the cruiser was a mile distant, but everything pointed against it. The craft, which proved to be a small coasting schooner, had evidently seen a lot of trouble. Both masts were broken off, the foremast close to the deck and the mainmast some dozen feet above it. She lay low in the water, with her decks piled high with lumber. A tangle of spars and ropes hung astern, but save for her cargo the decks had been swept clean. She was a sad sight even at that distance, and more than one aboard the *Adventurer* felt the pathos of her.

"No sign of life," said Steve. "If anyone was aboard there'd be a signal flying. And the boats are all gone, too, although that wouldn't mean much in itself because they might have been swept away. I guess, though, it got a bit too strenuous and the crew remembered the 'Safety First' slogan. There's nothing we can do, anyway."

He started to swing the cruiser about again, but Perry intervened. "She's a whatyoucallit!" he exclaimed excitedly. "She's -"

"No, little one," Joe corrected gently, "she's a wreck."

"She's a derelict," persisted Perry eagerly, "and no one belongs to her! If we got her she'd belong to us, Steve! Wouldn't she?"

"I suppose she would," replied Steve dubiously, his hand hesitating on the wheel, "but finding her and getting her are two mighty different things, Perry. If we *could* get her she'd be a nice prize, I guess, for lumber's worth real money these days, and although she isn't very big it's safe to say she's got quite a bunch of it on her, below deck and above. I guess that lumber is what kept her afloat, from the looks of the hull."

"Let's see what we can do," said Han. "Someone will find her and -"

"It might as well be us," added Perry enthusiastically. "Couldn't we tow her, Steve!"

"Tow her! Gee, she'd follow about as easily as a brick house!"

"But if we both pulled -"

"Well" - Steve cast an appraising eye at the weather - "I'm game to try it if the rest of you say so. Full steam ahead, Mr. Chapman!"

RALPH HENRY BARBOUR

CHAPTER XXI

ON BOARD THE *CATSPAW*

Steve communicated the project to those aboard the *Follow Me* which had now drawn up as near as she dared, and there followed a moment of blank amazement aboard the smaller boat. But discussion there was brief, and almost at once Harry Corwin raised his megaphone again and bellowed across:

"Go to it! What do you want us to do, Steve?"

"Nothing yet," was the answer. "We're going to board her first and see how she looks. If we take on the job we'll want your heaviest cable."

Harry signalled assent. By this time they were within a hundred yards of the derelict, and, with engines just moving, they tossed about on the long swells and had a better look at the schooner. She was about eighty feet long, with a beam of probably twenty-two, and displaced approximately a hundred tons. She was square-sterned and blunt-nosed, evidently built for capacity rather than speed. Her name, in gold letters on the bow, was quite distinct: *Catspaw.* Later, when they rounded her stern, they saw that her home port was Norfolk. Her cargo, or at least so much of it as was above deck, consisted of rough pine boards, and every available foot of space was occupied with it. The deck-house was all but hidden. The mainmast dragged by a tangle of ropes aft of the starboard beam and was acting as a sort of sea-anchor. For the rest, her lumber-piled deck was swept clean save for a splintered gaff that had become wedged in the boards. Her hull had been painted black, but not very recently, and a dingy white streak led along the side.

The two cruisers worked cautiously around to the leeward side of the *Catspaw*, the *Adventurer's* tender was dropped over and Steve, Joe and Han climbed in. Boarding in that sea was no child's work, for the big swells, which slammed into and sometimes over the schooner without much effect, tossed the dingey high in air. But by rowing hard at first and then taking advantage of the quieter water near the schooner they at last reached the old black hull in safety and, while Han managed the boat-hook, the other two scrambled aboard.

As they had suspected, the hulk was utterly deserted, and the fact that the forecastle and the captain's quarters were bare of anything of value and that the davits were empty indicated that the vessel had been abandoned in order. There was a good deal of water in her, but, as Steve pointed out, she wouldn't sink in a dozen years with that load of lumber to hold her up. "She wouldn't show much speed," he said when they had completed their investigations and were once more on deck, "and she'll tow about as easy as a lump of lead, but it's only thirty miles or so to Portsmouth, and even if we make only two miles an hour, and I guess we won't make much more, we can get her there tomorrow. That is, we can if our cables hold and the weather doesn't get nasty. I don't much like the looks of that same weather, though."

"Well, the barometer is rising," said Joe, "and that means -"

"Never mind your old barometer," laughed Steve. "Anyway, we'll have a go at this. If we have to give it up, all right, but we'd be silly not to try it. Come on and we'll get the cables aboard."

Two hours of hard work followed. With the cruisers tagging along nearby, suiting their pace to the slow drift of the schooner, the boys cut away the wreckage and rigged a jury-mast at the stump of the foremast. On this they spread a spare forestaysail which they dug from the sail locker. That it would aid greatly in the ship's progress Steve did not expect, but it would, he figured, make steering easier. Then the cruiser's heaviest anchor cables were taken aboard and made fast at the bow. A "prize crew" consisting of Joe, Han and Perry, from the *Adventurer*, and Wink and Bert, from the *Follow Me*, was placed in charge and enough food for two meals supplied them. The galley stove was still in running order, although it reeked of grease, and there was a fair supply of wood handy. Bert Alley, who had volunteered to do the cooking, objected to an inch or so of water that swashed around the floor, but the others pulled a pair of old rubber boots from a chest in the forecastle and he became reconciled. At noon they all returned to their respective cruisers and ate dinner, which, under the conditions, was no easy matter. They had to hold the dishes to the table and swallow their tea between plunges. Joe was inordinately proud of himself that day, for, in spite of the nasty motion - and there's nothing much more likely to induce sickness than a long ground-swell - he not only remained on duty but consumed his dinner with a fine appetite. It rained quite hard for a half-hour about noon and then ceased just in time for them to set off to the *Catspaw* again. It was decided that the *Follow Me's* tender was to be left with the schooner, in case of necessity, and Joe acknowledged that he felt a bit easier in his mind when it had been hoisted, not without difficulty, to one of the davits.

"It's all fine and dandy to say that this old tub can't sink," he confided to Wink Wheeler, "but - um - suppose she *did* sink? Then that little old dingey would be worth about a thousand dollars, I guess."

"It would be worth about ten cents," answered Wink pessimistically, "after we'd crowded five fellows into her in a sea like this!"

"Well, anyway, she's bigger than ours," said Joe. "And I saw a life belt downstairs - I mean below."

Joe and Wink were to take watches at the wheel, Perry and

Han were to tend to the sail and keep a lookout and Bert was to cook. Steve issued his final directions at a little past one and then the two hawsers were stretched to the cruisers. Another squall of rain set in as the final preparations were made. A code of signals had been arranged between the three boats, a flag or piece of sailcloth to be used while the light held and a lantern after darkness. The "prize crew" cheered gaily as the others pulled away in the *Adventurer's* dingey and were cheered in return, and five minutes later the two cables tautened, the water foamed under the overhangs of the motor-boats and, reluctantly and even protestingly, the *Catspaw* obeyed the summons and started slowly to follow in the wakes of the distant cruisers.

Han and Perry, at the bow, waved caps triumphantly as the blunt nose of the schooner began to dig into the waves, and Joe, at the wheel, shouted back. The three-cornered sail was shifted to meet the following breeze and soon the *Catspaw* was wallowing along slowly but, as it seemed, in a determined way at the rate of, perhaps, three miles an hour. Perry, protected by a slicker, seated himself on the windlass and felt very important. Now and then someone aboard one of the cruisers waved a hand and Perry waved superbly back. Those cruisers were a long way off in case of danger, he reflected once, but he decided not to let his mind dwell on the fact.

Joe found that the wheel of the *Catspaw* required a good deal more attention than that of the *Adventurer*, and his arms were fairly tired by the time he yielded his place to the impatiently eager Wink. Steering the *Catspaw* with the sea almost up to her deck line was a good deal like steering a scow loaded with pig-iron, Joe decided. Not, of course, that he had ever steered a scow of any sort, but he had imagination.

The *Adventurer* and *Follow Me* were heading West Southwest one-fourth West to pass Boon Island to starboard, and Kittery Point lay some thirty miles away. As it was then just short of three bells, and as they were making, as near as those aboard the *Catspaw* could judge, very nearly three miles an hour, it seemed probable that by two o'clock that night they would be at anchor off Portsmouth Harbour. Of course, there was always the possibility of bad weather or a broken cable, but the *Catspaw's* crew declined to be pessimistic. They were having a royal good time. There was enough danger in the enterprise to make it exciting, and, being normal, healthy chaps, excitement was better than food. Perry proclaimed his delight at last finding an adventure quite to his taste.

"Being wrecked on that island the other day was poor fun," he declared. "And it was dreadfully messy, too. But this is the real thing, fellows! Why, this old hooker might take it into her head to go down *ker-plop* any minute!"

"Huh," replied Wink Wheeler, "that may be your idea of the real thing, Perry, but it isn't mine. I'm just as strong for adventure as you, sonny, but I prefer mine on top of the water and not underneath!"

"Shucks," said Joe, "this thing can't sink. Look at all the lumber on her!"

"Yes, but it might get water-logged," suggested Bert from the door of the deck-house. "Wood does, doesn't it?"

"Not for a long time," said Joe. "Years, maybe. And this lumber's new. You can tell by the looks of it."

"Well, don't be to sure," advised Perry, darkly. "You never can tell. And there's another thing, too. We're top-heavy, with all these boards piled up on deck here, and if a storm came up we might easily turn turtle."

"Oh, dry up," said Han. "You're worse than Poe's raven. Besides, she couldn't turn over, you idiot, as long as the lumber floated. She'd have to stay right-side up."

"Wish we had a barometer aboard," said Joe. "We'd know what to expect then."

"You mean we'd know what you'd tell us to expect," replied Perry ironically. "And then we'd get something else. For my part, I'm glad they took their old barometer with them."

"They took about everything that wasn't nailed down except the stove," said Wink.

"That's nailed down, too," said Bert. "Or, at least, it's bolted. How many do you suppose there were on board when the storm hit them?"

"About five, maybe. Perhaps six. I guess five could handle a schooner this size. Five are handling her now, anyway," Joe added.

Nothing of moment occurred during the afternoon, if we except occasional squalls of rain, until, at about five, those on the schooner observed a smudge of smoke to the southward that eventually proved to be coming from an ocean tug. The tug approached them half an hour later and ran alongside the *Adventurer*. The boys on the *Catspaw* saw the boat's captain appear from the pilot-house and point a megaphone toward the white cruiser, and glimpsed Steve replying. What was said they could only surmise, but the tug's mission was evident enough.

"He wants the job," said Joe anxiously. "Wonder if Steve will let him have it."

"I hope he doesn't," said Wink. "We can do the trick without anyone's help, I guess. Besides, he'd want half the money we'll get."

"More than half, probably," said Han. "He's still talking. I wish he'd run away smiling."

He did finally. That is, he went off, but whether he was smiling they couldn't say. They fancied, however, that he was not, for the *Catspaw* would have made a nice prize for the

RALPH HENRY BARBOUR

tug's owners.

The tug plunged off the way she had come and was soon only a speck in the gathering twilight. It seemed a bit more lonesome after she had gone, and more than one of the quintette aboard the *Catspaw* wondered whether, after all, it might not have been the part of wisdom to have accepted assistance. Darkness came early that evening, and by six the lights on the *Adventurer* and *Follow Me* showed wanly across the surly, shadowy sea. Han and Perry had already prepared the two lanterns they had found on board and as soon as the cruisers set the fashion they placed them fore and aft, one where it could be plainly seen from the boats ahead and the other on the roof of the deck-house. While they were at that task the darkness settled down rapidly, and by the time they had finished the cruisers were only blotches against which shone the white lights placed at the sterns for the guidance of the *Catspaw's* navigators.

The boys ate their suppers in relays about half-past six. Bert had prepared plenty of coffee and cooked several pans of bacon and eggs, and had done very well for a tyro. Later the *Adventurer* turned on her searchlight and against the white path of it she was plainly visible. A more than usually severe squall of wind and rain broke over them about eight and when the rain, which pelted quite fiercely for a few minutes, had passed on the wind continued. It was coming from the northwest and held a chilliness that made the amateur mariners squirm down into their sweaters and raincoats. The *Catspaw*, low in the water as she was, nevertheless felt the push of the wind and keeping her blunt nose pointed midway between the two lights ahead became momentarily more difficult. At the end of an hour it required the services of both Joe and Wink to hold the schooner steady. Perry and Han, huddled as much out of the chilling wind as they could be, kept watch at the bow. Keeping watch, though, was more a figure of speech than an actuality, for the night was intensely dark and save for the lights of the towing craft nothing was discernible.

The sea arose under the growing strength of the nor'wester and soon the waves were thudding hard against the rail and the piled lumber and sending showers of spray across the deck. The *Catspaw* rolled and wallowed and the watchers at the bow soon knew from the sound of the straining cables that the cruisers were having difficulty. Bert crawled forward through the darkness and spray and joined them.

"Joe says they'll be signalling to cast off the hawsers pretty quick," he bellowed above the wind and waves. "He says we aren't making any headway at all now."

"Gee, it'll be fine to be left pitching around here all night," said Perry alarmedly. "If we only had an anchor -"

"I'd rather keep on drifting," said Han. "It'll be a lot more comfortable."

"Maybe, but we'll be going out to sea again. Seems to me they might keep hold of us even if they don't get along much." Perry ducked before the hissing avalanche of spray that was flung across the deck. "There's one thing certain," he added despondently. "We've got to stay on this old turtle as long as she'll let us, for we couldn't get that dingey off now if we tried!"

"What's the difference?" asked Han. "They'll stick around us until the wind goes down again, and we're just as well off here as they are on the boats. Bet you the *Adventurer* is doing some pitching herself about now!"

They relapsed into silence then, for making one's self heard above the clamour of wind and water and the groans and creakings of the schooner was hard work. They watched the *Adventurer* for the expected signal for a long time, but it was nearly ten when a lantern began to swing from side to side on the cruiser. A moment later they heard faintly the shriek of the *Adventurer's* whistle.

RALPH HENRY BARBOUR

CHAPTER XXII

INTO PORT

"Cast off!" said Han. "Take this one first, Perry. Gee, but it's stiff!" They had to fumble several minutes at the wet cable before they got it clear and let it slip over the bow. Then the other was cast off as well and Bert swung the lantern four times above his head as a signal to haul in. An answering dip of the light on the stern of the *Adventurer* answered, just as Joe joined them.

"All right?" he asked anxiously.

"Yes, both clear," replied Han. "What do we do now, Joe?"

"Sit tight and wait. Some of us had better get some sleep. Perry, you and Bert might as well turn in for awhile. I'm going to. It's ten o'clock. I'll wake you at two, and you can relieve Han. Bert, you might make some coffee when you tumble out again. We'll probably need it."

"I'm not sleepy a bit," protested Perry. But Joe insisted and he and Bert followed the other below and laid down in the bunks in the captain's cabin. In spite of his disclaimer and the noise and rolling of the ship, Perry was asleep almost as soon as he touched the berth, and the others were not far behind.

Joe had the faculty of waking up at any predetermined hour, and at two he was shaking the others from their slumbers. It was at once evident that the gale had increased, for it was all they could do to keep their feet under them as they made their way to the galley. Bert set about making a fire while the others made their way to the wheel. Wink greeted them cheerfully enough from the lantern-lit darkness there, but his voice sounded weary in spite of him.

"I had Han take the sail down," he announced. "She steers better without it. The wind's pretty fierce, isn't it? Look out!"

A big wave broke over the rail and descended on them in bucketfulls.

"That's what makes it so pleasant," shouted Wink. "Guess I'll take a nap if I can."

"Bert's making some coffee," said Joe. "Better have some before you turn in."

Perry made his way cautiously forward and relieved Han. "Seen anything?" he asked.

"Not a thing."

"Hello, where are the boats?" Perry stared ahead in surprise.

"One of them - I think it's the *Adventurer* - is back there." Han turned Perry about until he glimpsed a faint flicker of light far off over the starboard beam. "Don't know where the other is. Guess they're having a rough time of it."

"I'll bet!" agreed Perry. "You're to have some coffee and turn in, Han."

"Coffee!" murmured the other gratefully. "Have you had some?"

"No, I'll get mine later. Beat it, you!"

Han disappeared in the darkness and Perry, wrapping himself as best he could in the folds of his slicker, settled himself to his task. Now and then he looked back for a glimpse of the friendly light at the stern or for sight of the *Adventurer*. The wind made strange whistling sounds through the interstices of the lumber and the battered hull groaned and creaked rheumatically. When he stood erect the gale tore at him frantically, and at all times the spray, dashing across the deck, kept him running with water. He grew frightfully sleepy about three and had difficulty in keeping awake. In spite of his efforts his head would sink and at last he had to walk the few paces he could manage, accommodating his uncertain steps to the roll of the boat, in order to defeat slumber.

To say that Perry did not more than once regret his suggestion of rescuing the *Catspaw* would be far from the truth. He felt very lonely out there on that bow, and his stomach was none too happy. And the thought of what would happen to him and the others if the schooner decided to give up the struggle was not at all pleasant to dwell on. And so he did his best not to think about it, but he didn't always succeed. On the whole it was a very miserable three hours that he spent on lookout duty that night. Once Bert crawled forward and shared his loneliness, but didn't remain very long, preferring the partial shelter of the house. No one was ever much gladder to see the sky lighten in the east than was Perry that morning. But even when a grey dawn had settled over the ocean the surroundings were not much more cheerful. As Wink said, it was a bit better to drown by daylight than to do it in the dark, but, aside from the fact that the *Catspaw* was still afloat, there wasn't much to be thankful for.

One of the cruisers was barely visible off to the northward, but the other was nowhere in sight. The grey-green waves looked mountain-high when seen from the water-washed deck of the *Catspaw*, and the wind, while seeming to have passed its wildest stage, still blew hard. There was no sight of land in any direction and Joe pessimistically decided that they were then some forty miles at sea and about off the Isles of Shoals. Soon after the sun had come up, somewhere behind the leaden clouds, they sighted a brig to the southward. She was hardly hull-up and was making her way under almost bare yards toward the west. She stayed in sight less than half an hour.

The boys had breakfast about half-past six. Except coffee and bread there was little left, and the outlook, in case the gale continued, was not inspiring! Perry declared that he'd much rather drown than starve to death. The first cheerful event that happened was the drawing near of the *Adventurer*. The white cruiser came plunging up to within a quarter of a mile about nine o'clock and signals were exchanged. An hour later the *Follow Me* appeared coming up from westward and at noon the schooner and the two convoys were reunited. But there was still no chance of getting lines aboard. All that they could do was wait. Dinner hour aboard the *Catspaw* was dinner hour in name only. There was coffee, to be sure, but the sugar was low and the condensed milk had given out completely. All else had disappeared at breakfast time. The spirits of the "prize crew" got lower and lower as the afternoon began and they were faced with another night aboard the schooner. Twice they sighted other craft, once a steamer headed toward the north-east and once a schooner dipping along under reefed sails. Neither craft showed any curiosity and each went on its way without a sign.

Once the *Adventurer* circled close to the windward and Steve shouted encouragement through his megaphone. Just what was said they couldn't make out, and Joe's attempts to acquaint the cruiser with the fact that they were out of provisions was unsuccessful, since he had only his hands to shout through and the wind was unsympathetic. But having the cruisers at hand was comforting, and when, at about four, there was a brief glimpse of sunlight to the south their spirits arose somewhat. The wind now began to go down perceptibly and by five it no longer roared down on them from the northwest, but, swinging around to the northeast, became quite docile and friendly. They put up their sail again and gradually the *Catspaw* pointed her nose toward the coast. Just before darkness came the sea had quieted enough to make possible an attempt to get the cables aboard again and those on the schooner saw the cruisers draw together. Steve and Phil caught the line hurled from the *Follow Me* after several attempts and then the tender was dropped over and with the two cables aboard the boys made for the *Catspaw*.

Those on the schooner watched anxiously. At one moment the tiny dingey was seen poised on the summit of a great green sea and the next was quite gone from sight. The sun came out momentarily before saying Good Night, as though to watch that struggle. At last the tender came sidling down the slope of a wave, the occupants striving hard at the oars, and after one breathless moment, during which it seemed that the little boat would be crushed to splinters against the old black hull of the schooner, Joe caught the painter, Steve made a flying leap for the deck and gained it in safety, and Phil, boat-hook in hand, worked manfully and skilfully to fend off while the cables were brought aboard. The dingey had fetched food as well and a shout of joy went up as Phil, taking advantage of the calm moments between the rushing waves, hurled the bundles to the deck.

There was little time for conversation, for darkness was coming fast, but Steve heard a brief account of the *Catspaw's* experiences, and, while helping to make fast the cables, told of the night aboard the *Adventurer*. "It was fierce," Steve said. "No one had much sleep, I guess. We almost pitched on our nose time and again. If it hadn't been for you chaps we'd have cut and run about midnight. We lost sight of your lights several times; they were so low in the water, and thought that you'd gone down at first. The *Follow Me* had to run for it, and I guess they weren't very happy either. But we'll make it this time. It's clearing up nicely and we're only forty miles from Portsmouth. Keep your lips stiff, fellows, and we'll be eating breakfast ashore!"

The dingey pulled off again, narrowly escaping capsizing more than once, and ten minutes afterwards the *Catspaw* was once more wallowing along in the wake of the cruisers. Supper, with bacon and potatoes and lots of bread, perked the crew up mightily, and when the stars began to peep through the scudding clouds and the sea stopped tormenting the poor old *Catspaw* they got quite cheerful. That second night was an easy one for all hands. The weather cleared entirely by two o'clock and the sea calmed to almost normal conditions. The *Catspaw* strained along at the ends of the cables at about three miles an hour until she got close enough to the shore to feel the tide. After that she went more slowly. At early dawn - and it was a real dawn this time, with sunlight on the water and a golden glow in the eastern sky - the Isles of Shoals lay six miles to the southwest and the blue shore line was beckoning them. At a little before eleven that forenoon the *Catspaw* passed Portsmouth Light and half an hour later, having been given over to the care of a tug, was lying snugly against a wharf.

It was a tired but triumphant dozen that stretched their legs ashore at noon and set out in search of dinner. Already they had answered a score of questions and told their story half a dozen times, and even after they were seated at table in the best restaurant that the city afforded - and it was a very good restaurant, too - an enterprising newspaper reporter found them out and Steve, as spokesman, recounted their adventures once more between mouthfuls.

And when at last they could eat no more and the reporter had gone off to write his story, Steve, Joe and Wink set forth to an address they had secured on the wharf and the others adjourned to the porch of a nearby hotel to await their return. "Tell him," instructed Perry as they parted, "that we won't accept a cent less than a thousand dollars! And," he added to himself, "I wouldn't go through it again for fifty thousand!"

CHAPTER XXIII

SALVAGE

Mr. Anthony T. Hyatt, attorney-at-law, leaned smilingly back in a swivel-chair, matched ten pudgy fingers together and smiled expansively at his clients. There was a great deal of Mr. Hyatt, and much of it lay directly behind his clasped hands. He had a large, round face in the centre of which a small, sharp nose surmounted a wide mouth and was flanked by a pair of pale brown eyes at once innocent and shrewd. Steve counted three chins and was not certain there wasn't another tucked away behind the collar of the huge shirt. Mr. Hyatt had a deep and mellow voice, and his words rolled and rumbled out like the reverberations of a good-natured thunder storm. From the windows of the bright, breeze-swept office the boys could look far out to sea, and it was possible that the faintly nautical atmosphere that appertained both to the office and its occupant was due to the sight and smell of the salt water. While Steve told his story the lawyer's expression slowly changed from jovial amusement to surprise, and when the narrative was ended he drew himself ponderously from the chair and rolled to a window.

"You say you've got her tied up to Sawyer's Wharf, eh?" he asked.

"Yes, sir."

"I want to know! Well! Well! Where'd you say you came across her?" Steve told him again. "And you brought her in yourself, eh?"

"The lot of us did. Now what we want to know is what claim have we got against the owners, Mr. Hyatt?"

The lawyer heaved himself back to his chair and lowered himself into it with what the boys thought was a most reckless disregard of the article's capacity and strength. But the chair only creaked dismally. "Of course you do! Of course you do!" he rumbled smilingly. "But s'posing I was to tell you you hadn't any claim at all on 'em?"

"What! No claim at all?" exclaimed Steve.

The man laughed and shook. "I only said s'posing," he protested. He weaved his fingers together again over his ample stomach. "As a matter of law, young gentlemen, you have an excellent claim, a steel-bound, double-riveted claim. Whether it's against the owners or some insurance company is what you'll have to find out first. Most likely that ship and cargo were insured. As to just what amount you are entitled to, the law doesn't state. That's a matter generally agreed on between the salvors and the owners. When no agreement can be reached the case goes to the Admiralty Court."

"Oh," said Steve. "The first thing to do -"

"I guess the first thing to do is find out who the owners are and see what they have to say. If they make you a fair offer, well and good. Now, do you want me to take this case for you?"

"Why, yes, sir, I think so," replied Steve, glancing inquiringly at the others, who nodded assent. "How much - that is, what -"

"What would I charge you for my services?" boomed the lawyer. "Nothing at all, boys, unless you get a settlement. If we don't have to go to court you may pay me a hundred dollars. If we do, we'll make another arrangement later. That satisfactory?"

"Yes, indeed," answered Steve heartily, and the rest murmured agreement. "How long will it take to find out, sir?"

"I'll have the owner's name in half an hour. Then I'll send them a wire. You drop in tomorrow at this time and I dare say I'll have something to tell you. I'll have a look at the boat this afternoon and get an idea of her value as a bottom. Then we'll get someone to give an estimate on her cargo. Would you be willing to pay ten dollars for an appraisement?"

"Yes, sir, if that's advisable."

"Well, I think it is. We'd better know what we've got, eh? All right, gentlemen. You leave it to me. Where are you stopping?"

"We're staying aboard our boats, sir, the *Adventurer* and the *Follow Me.*"

"I want to know! Regular mariners, ain't ye? Well! Well! Guess you're having a fine time, too, eh?"

"Yes, sir, we've had a pretty good time. About - about how much do you think we ought to get for the boat, Mr. Hyatt?"

"Including cargo? Well, now, I don't know, Mister - What did you say your name is?"

"Stephen Chapman."

"Mr. Stephen Chapman, eh?" The lawyer wrote it on a scrap of paper and thrust it carelessly into a pigeon-hole of the old walnut desk. "Well, there ought to be a tidy sum coming to you, sir; yes, sir, a tidy sum. Lumber is fetching money just now, and you tell me the *Catspaw* is loaded high."

"Yes, sir, she's loaded up to her rails. Do you suppose we'll get a thousand dollars?"

"A thousand dollars, eh?" Mr. Hyatt beamed broadly and

nodded until all his chins in sight shook. "Yes, you might look for a thousand dollars, boys. It isn't sense to get your expectations too high, but I guess you can safely bank on a thousand. Oh, yes, a thousand isn't unreasonable. Well, you drop around tomorrow and maybe there'll be something to report. I'll get right to work, gentlemen. Good afternoon!"

"Funny old whale, isn't he?" commented Joe when they were once more on the street. "Suppose he knows what he's talking about?"

"Why not?" asked Wink. "He struck me as being rather a canny customer."

"Well, he said a thousand dollars," replied Joe. "That's a lot of money, isn't it, for an old schooner like the *Catspaw*?"

"It isn't much for the schooner and the cargo, too," said Steve. "I'm wondering if it oughtn't to be a lot more; say fifteen hundred. You see, a schooner like that costs quite a lot of money when it's new. And then, as Mr. Hyatt said, lumber is high right now, and there's a pile of it on board."

"A thousand will suit me all right," said Joe. "A twelfth of a thousand is - is -"

"A thirteenth you mean," corrected Steve. "Don't forget Neil."

"And don't count your chickens until they're hatched," Wink advised. "It's unlucky, Joe."

They found the other members of the expedition in various states of coma induced by a hearty dinner and lack of sleep, but they were all wide awake when Steve announced the result of the visit to the lawyer.

"Gee!" exclaimed "Brownie." "A thousand dollars! He's fooling, isn't he? Why, I thought we'd get maybe three hundred!"

"A thousand isn't a cent too much," said Perry. "Come to think of it, fellows, I earned that much myself!"

"Just a minute, fellows," said Steve, interrupting the jeers that greeted Perry's statement. "What are we going to do with the money when we get it?"

There was a moment of silence. Then Tom Corwin inquired: "Do with it? How do you mean, do with it, Steve? I thought it would be divided up pro rata."

"Of course," agreed Cas and Ossie in unison.

"Wait a minute," said Phil. "Steve's got something on his mind. Let's hear it."

Steve swung himself to the porch rail and faced the half-circle of boys. "It's just an idea," he began, "and if you don't like it you've only got to say so. As I look at it, fellows, this club has been a good deal of a success. If we haven't had any whopping big adventures, we've had some mild ones -"

"Great Jumping Jehoshaphat!" muttered Han. "What do you call adventures?"

Steve smiled and went on, "At any rate, we've had a whole lot of fun. At least, I have." He looked about him inquiringly.

"You bet we have!" answered Joe heartily, and the rest echoed him.

"Of course, we got the club up just for this Summer, I suppose, but I don't see any reason why we shouldn't make it a - a permanent affair."

"Bully!" exclaimed Perry. "Second the motion!"

"Sit down!" growled Wink.

"There's next Summer coming, fellows. We could do something like this again if we wanted to. We needn't make a trip in motor-boats, but we could do something just as good. Well, now, why not take this money when we get it and stow it away in the Club treasury instead of spending it? Then we'd have enough to do almost anything we liked next year. If we each got our seventy-seven dollars, or whatever the shares might be, we'd have it spent in a month and never know where it got to. But if we put it in the bank at interest we'd - we'd have something. If you don't like the scheme, just say so. I'm willing to do whatever the rest of you say, only I thought -"

"It's a corking idea," declared Harry Corwin enthusiastically. "You're dead right, Steve, too. Seventy-seven dollars would last about two weeks with me. Why hang it, I've had it spent ten times already, and each time for some fool thing I didn't really want! I say, let's keep the Club going, fellows, and put the money in the treasury. And let Phil deposit it in a bank. At four per cent, or whatever it is banks pay you, it would come to nearly - nearly thirty dollars by next Summer. And thirty dollars would buy us gasoline for a month!"

"Right you are," agreed Wink. "We'll make a real club of it."

"How about the rest of you?" asked Steve.

The others were all in favour, although Perry couldn't quite smother a sigh of regret for the cash in hand he had dreamed of, and there followed an enthusiastic discussion of plans for next Summer, and Bert Alley echoed the sentiment of all when he remarked regretfully that next Summer was an awfully long way off! Ossie made the suggestion that it might be a good plan to reimburse the members from the salvage money for what sums they had expended on the present cruise, explaining, however, that he wasn't particular on his own account. The question was argued and finally decided in the negative. As Phil put it, what they had spent would have been spent in any case, whether they had gone on the cruise or stayed at home, and they had all received full value for their contributions. Still planning, they went back to the boats and spent the rest of the afternoon in cleaning them up inside and out, for both the *Adventurer* and the *Follow Me* had been sadly neglected for the past forty-eight hours.

Being persons of wealth, they supped ashore and went to a moving picture show, and afterwards, since no one had had his full allowance of sleep for the past two nights, "hit the hay," in Perry's phraseology, in short order and slept like so many logs until sun-up.

"I wish," remarked Han at breakfast the next morning, "that we were just starting out instead of going home."

"Me too," agreed Perry. "It'll be all over in two or three days, and I'll have to go back to school again. I suppose," he added sadly, "I shan't see any of you fellows again until next Summer; no one but Ossie, that is."

"You don't have to look at me if you don't want to," said Ossie, reaching backward into the galley for the coffee-pot. "I'm not particular."

"You'll see us before Summer," replied Steve. "I've been thinking."

"So that's it , " murmured Joe. "I thought maybe you just - um - hadn't slept well."

"If we're going to keep the Club together," continued Steve, treating the interruption disdainfully, "we've got to keep in touch with each other. Suppose now we have a meeting about Christmas time, during vacation."

"Good scheme!" applauded Phil.

"I think so. My idea is to keep out about thirty dollars of that money, or take it out later, I suppose, and have a feed some-where, a sort of Annual Banquet of the Adventure Club of

America, not Incorporated. We could hold a business meeting first and then feed our faces and talk over this Summer's fun and have a jolly old time. What do you say! Pass the sugar, Han."

They said many things, but they were all in praise of the idea, and later the *Follow Me's* contingent was quite as enthusiastic, and Steve, in his official capacity of Number One, finally found a calendar and solemnly announced that Saturday, the twenty-third day of December, was the date, that the hour was six o'clock, post meredian, and that the place would be decided on later. After which they all went ashore and passed the time until dinner in various ways. And at a little before two Steve, Joe and Wink once more climbed the narrow stairway to Lawyer Hyatt's office.

"I have here," said Mr. Hyatt, when they had seated themselves and greetings had been exchanged and the weather duly and thoroughly disposed of, "a telegram from Barrows and Leland, of Norfolk, Virginia, agents for the owners of the schooner *Catspaw*. In it they make an offer of settlement of your claim, subject, of course, to the facts and conditions being as stated in my telegram to them."

He paused impressively and the boys shuffled their feet in silent expectancy.

"Hm. Now I'm not going to advise you to accept their offer and I'm not going to advise you not to," he rumbled. "Only, I do say this, gentlemen. If you take your case to the Admiralty Court it will cost you a good deal of money and you won't get a final judgment for a long time. Of course, you might, in the end, get a better figure. I'd almost be willing to guarantee that you would. But you want to remember that the costs of a trial aren't small and that they might eat a big hole in the difference between the present offer and the court's award."

"What - what do they offer us?" asked Steve as the lawyer paused to clear his throat.

"There's no doubt that the value of the *Catspaw* and her cargo is a sight more than these fellows offer us," resumed Mr. Hyatt, quite as though he had not heard the question. "But there's the old adage about a bird on toast being worth more than a bird on the telegraph wire." He chuckled deeply. "And, of course, no owner ever thinks of paying the full value of salvaged property. Nor does the court expect him to. Something like an equable division is what they try to award."

"Yes, sir," murmured Steve nervously. "Yes, sir. Would you mind -"

"You said something yesterday about a thousand dollars, and I told you you might expect that much, didn't I?"

Steve nodded silently.

"Well -" The lawyer took up a sheet of creased yellow paper from the desk and ran his eyes along the message thereon. "Well, I've got to tell you they don't offer you a thousand, boys."

"Oh!" murmured Steve.

"Don't they?" gasped Joe weakly.

"Then what -" began Wink dejectedly.

"They offer you -" Mr. Hyatt leaned forward in the protesting chair and held the telegram toward Steve - "they offer you four thousand, seven hundred and sixty-one dollars, young gentlemen."

*　　*　　*　　*　　*

Isn't this a good place to end our story? I might tell how they wired the good news to Neil, and how they set forth that afternoon for New York, and how, after a jolly but uneventful trip, the two boats parted company off Bay Shore, and how the

Adventurer, having done her best to deserve the name she bore, at last sidled up to a slip in the yacht basin and discharged her crew. And I might depict the awed delight with which, two days later, Steve, Joe and Phil gazed upon a narrow strip of green paper bearing the wonderful legend "Four Thousand Seven Hundred Sixty-one Dollars." But we set out in search of adventures, and we have reached the last of them, and so the chronicle should end. And since it began with a remark from Perry let us end it so. Perry's closing remark was made from the platform of the train for Philadelphia.

"Good-bye, you fellows," said Perry, smiling widely to show that he didn't mind leaving the others the least bit in the world. "We had a corking good time, didn't we? But just let me tell you something. It isn't a patch on the fun we're going to have on the next trip of the Adventure Club!"

Choose from Thousands of 1stWorldLibrary Classics By

Adolphus WilliamWard
Aesop
Agatha Christie
Alexander Aaronsohn
Alexander Kielland
Alexandre Dumas
Alfred Gatty
Alfred Ollivant
Alice Duer Miller
Alice Turner Curtis
Alice Dunbar
Ambrose Bierce
Amelia E. Barr
Andrew Lang
Andrew McFarland Davis
Anna Sewell
Annie Besant
Annie Hamilton Donnell
Annie Payson Call
Anton Chekhov
Arnold Bennett
Arthur Conan Doyle
Arthur Ransome
Atticus
B. M. Bower
Basil King
Bayard Taylor
Ben Macomber
Booth Tarkington
Bram Stoker
C. Collodi
C. E. Orr
C. M. Ingleby
Carolyn Wells
Catherine Parr Traill
Charles A. Eastman
Charles Dickens
Charles Dudley Warner
Charles Farrar Browne
Charles Ives
Charles Kingsley
Charles Lathrop Pack
Charles Whibley
Charles Willing Beale
Charlotte M. Braeme
Charlotte M.Yonge
Clair W. Hayes
Clarence Day Jr.
Clarence E. Mulford

Clemence Housman
Confucius
Cornelis DeWitt Wilcox
Cyril Burleigh
D. H. Lawrence
Daniel Defoe
David Garnett
Don Carlos Janes
Donald Keyhole
Dorothy Kilner
Dougan Clark
E. Nesbit
E.P.Roe
E. Phillips Oppenheim
Edgar Allan Poe
Edgar Rice Burroughs
Edith Wharton
Edward J. O'Biren
John Cournos
Edwin L. Arnold
Eleanor Atkins
Elizabeth Cleghorn
Gaskell
Elizabeth Von Arnim
Ellem Key
Emily Dickinson
Erasmus W. Jones
Ernie Howard Pie
Ethel Turner
Ethel Watts Mumford
Eugenie Foa
Eugene Wood
Evelyn Everett-Green
Everard Cotes
F. J. Cross
Federick Austin Ogg
Ferdinand Ossendowski
Francis Bacon
Francis Darwin
Frances Hodgson Burnett
Frank Gee Patchin
Frank Harris
Frank Jewett Mather
Frank L. Packard
Frederick Trevor Hill
Frederick Winslow Taylor
Friedrich Kerst
Friedrich Nietzsche
Fyodor Dostoyevsky

Gabrielle E. Jackson
Garrett P. Serviss
Gaston Leroux
George Ade
Geroge Bernard Shaw
George Ebers
George Eliot
George MacDonald
George Orwell
George Tucker
George W. Cable
George Wharton James
Gertrude Atherton
Grace E. King
Grant Allen
Guillermo A. Sherwell
Gulielma Zollinger
Gustav Flaubert
H. A. Cody
H. B. Irving
H. G. Wells
H. H. Munro
H. Irving Hancock
H. Rider Haggard
H. W. C. Davis
Hamilton Wright Mabie
Hans Christian Andersen
Harold Avery
Harold McGrath
Harriet Beecher Stowe
Harry Houidini
Helent Hunt Jackson
Helen Nicolay
Hendy David Thoreau
Henrik Ibsen
Henry Adams
Henry Ford
Henry Frost
Henry James
Henry Jones Ford
Henry Seton Merriman
Henry Wadsworth
Longfellow
Henry W Longfellow
Herbert A. Giles
Herbert N. Casson
Herman Hesse
Homer
Honore De Balzac

Horace Walpole
Horatio Alger, Jr.
Howard Pyle
Howard R. Garis
Hugh Lofting
Hugh Walpole
Humphry Ward
Ian Maclaren
Israel Abrahams
J.G.Austin
J. Henri Fabre
J. M. Barrie
J. Macdonald Oxley
J. S. Knowles
J. Storer Clouston
Jack London
Jacob Abbott
James Allen
James Lane Allen
James Andrews
James Baldwin
James DeMille
James Joyce
James Oliver Curwood
James Oppenheim
James Otis
Jane Austen
Jens Peter Jacobsen
Jerome K. Jerome
John Burroughs
John F. Kennedy
John Gay
John Glasworthy
John Habberton
John Joy Bell
John Milton
John Philip Sousa
Jonathan Swift
Joseph Carey
Joseph Conrad
Joseph Jacobs
Julian Hawthrone
Julies Vernes
Justin Huntly McCarthy
Kakuzo Okakura
Kenneth Grahame
Kate Langley Bosher
L. A. Abbot
L. T. Meade
L. Frank Baum
Laura Lee Hope

Laurence Housman
Leo Tolstoy
Leonid Andreyev
Lewis Carroll
Lilian Bell
Lloyd Osbourne
Louis Tracy
Louisa May Alcott
Lucy Fitch Perkins
Lucy Maud Montgomery
Lydia Miller Middleton
Lyndon Orr
M. H. Adams
Margaret E. Sangster
Margaret Vandercook
Maria Edgeworth
Maria Thompson Daviess
Mariano Azuela
Marion Polk Angellotti
Mark Overton
Mark Twain
Mary Austin
Mary Cole
Mary Rowlandson
Mary Wollstonecraft
Shelley
Max Beerbohm
Myra Kelly
Nathaniel Hawthrone
O. F. Walton
Oscar Wilde
Owen Johnson
P.G.Wodehouse
Paul and Mable Thorn
Paul G. Tomlinson
Paul Severing
Peter B. Kyne
Plato
R. Derby Holmes
R. L. Stevenson
Rabindranath Tagore
Rahul Alvares
Ralph Waldo Emmerson
Rene Descartes
Rex E. Beach
Richard Harding Davis
Richard Jefferies
Robert Barr
Robert Frost
Robert Gordon Anderson
Robert L. Drake

Robert Lansing
Robert Michael Ballantyne
Robert W. Chambers
Rosa Nouchette Carey
Ross Kay
Rudyard Kipling
Samuel B. Allison
Samuel Hopkins Adams
Sarah Bernhardt
Selma Lagerlof
Sherwood Anderson
Sigmund Freud
Standish O'Grady
Stanley Weyman
Stella Benson
Stephen Crane
Stewart Edward White
Stijn Streuvels
Swami Abhedananda
Swami Parmananda
T. S. Ackland
The Princess Der Ling
Thomas A. Janvier
Thomas A Kempis
Thomas Anderton
Thomas Bailey Aldrich
Thomas Bulfinch
Thomas De Quincey
Thomas H. Huxley
Thomas Hardy
Thomas More
Thornton W. Burgess
U. S. Grant
Valentine Williams
Victor Appleton
Virginia Woolf
Walter Scott
Washington Irving
Wilbur Lawton
Wilkie Collins
Willa Cather
Willard F. Baker
William Makepeace
Thackeray
William W. Walter
Winston Churchill
Yei Theodora Ozaki
Young E. Allison
Zane Grey